Denise Phillips

Greenstone Island

To my mother Beryl, my children Jordan and
Jamie-Leigh and my niece Carly Anne

Chapter One

A waiter dressed in a white uniform, walked through a lavishly set banqueting hall holding a solid silver tray aloft. On the silver tray were eight crystal glasses containing champagne. He weaved between the ten round tables each identically set with white linen tablecloths, white logoed napkins, white porcelain dining sets with gold rims, solid silver cutlery and crystal wine glasses. Each table also had a centrepiece bouquet of white orchids. The seated men were dressed in black jackets, white shirts and bow ties, the women in elegant evening dresses wearing expensive jewelry. In one corner of the hall, a string quartet played Vivaldi's Four Seasons. The event was in celebration of John Bosman CEO a.k.a Boss of South America Gems Inc. receiving the prestigious South America Businessman of the Year Award 1978, six months previously. The celebration was being held at the head office in Caracas. It was one of five offices owned by the firm throughout South America.

When the waiter arrived at his destination, he served the eight seated occupants. Taking a sip of the Dom Perignon, (champagne was not Ned's favourite tipple, but it would do for now) Ned looked around the hall. At the furthest side of the hall, beyond the other nine tables, were some high double fronted doors which were wide open... for the time being. As people walked past the doors on the other side, Ned spotted Felipe from the Administration's Department. Ned couldn't miss Felipe; he was wearing a salmon pink suit. Ned also observed a group of women standing next to a buffet table, chatting together. He knew some of the faces from his visits to the typing pool to deliver work. He was hoping to see Maggie and Lola, his two favourite typists with whom he had a laugh and a joke the odd days he visited head office. To Ned, these were real people, people without their heads buried in office politics and boring business chat. In the typing pool, Maggie, Lola and Ned would exchange stories about their lives, some funny and some sad. Lola would talk about her homeless experience before she joined the firm, Maggie about the orphanage where she spent her childhood years and Ned would talk about his time spent in England, where he grew up. Whenever Maggie and Lola saw Ned enter the typing department with some work, Lola would shout, "Look Maggie, it's Ned from the other side." The term 'other side' referred to the so-called 'important' people in the firm, the Directors, the Officers, anyone but the back-office staff. Looking further through the double doors towards the back of that room, Ned could just see a band preparing their instruments on a small stage.

Now and again he would hear the faint voice of a man at the front of the stage saying, "Testing, testing, testing," while simultaneously slapping a microphone.

Back in the banqueting hall, Ned observed the framed photographs hanging on the wall, various images of the firm mining fields in Chile, Venezuela, Colombia and Bolivia. But there was one main picture that stood out, that made Ned feel sick to the back teeth. It was the largest of all the photographs and set in a prime position for everyone in the hall to see. It was the one that made the front page of all South American newspapers 6 months previous to this event. It was a framed photograph of Boss holding a gold statue when he was awarded South America businessman of the year award 1978. He was the wealthiest man in South America, and the American who had received so much praise for improving the economy of South America. He who had built South America Gems Inc. from scratch, a point Ned was tired of hearing. And there he was in the photograph grinning like a dam Cheshire cat.

As Ned took another sip his thoughts went back to the hotel, where he had been prior to the event. Now, sitting at the table, he regretted drinking that bottle of red wine before coming to the event, the bottle of red which was a welcoming gift from the hotel. Ned and his Latino girlfriend Rosa had flown in from Bogotá, where the firm had a smaller office, earlier that day and booked into the hotel. While she was taking a long hot soak, Ned had been drinking straight from the bottle of wine. It didn't take Ned long to finish it and afterwards, what should have only been a ten-minute nap turned into an hour. That extra hour was the major factor in making the couple late to the event. Too late for Ned to swap the name place cards on his table with one of the other nine tables in the hall.

Ned took another sip and observed the bottles of wine on the table. Three expensive bottles of red and three expensive bottles of white, specially selected by Boss from a vineyard the firm owned in Tuscany. Ned secretly calculated in his head how long the six bottles would last between seven people, seven as Rosa did not drink, at least that is what he thought. Ned was always calculating things in his head. Sometimes he even thought he should have studied maths at University and not Geology. Opposite, through the array of orchids on the table sat two Americans, Jeff Walden, Chief Executive Officer of Marketing and Alan Parker, Chief Executive Officer of Finance. Ned recognized the two men from business meetings he'd had in this building and they represented the majority of men in the hall, successful, wealthy and middle aged. The men were also dressed in black dinner jackets, pristine white shirts and black bow ties and they each had a female companion. All four people opposite Ned were engrossed in deep conversation, and he overheard snippets now and then. The two women were looking around the seated occupants at the other nine tables discussing who's wearing what designer dress and whether it suited them or not. The men were talking about their private yachts in the South of France, making comparisons.

As Ned was about to take another sip, he spoke in a Texan droll.

"Well Ned, aren't you going to introduce me to your lovely lady companion?" Ned turned to his left to face him smoking his signature Havana cigar. He was John Bosman, CEO, also commonly known around the firm as simply Boss. Both he and Ned were showing signs of a middle-aged paunch but at least Ned still had a full head of hair, unlike his counterpart who was beginning to recede.

Ned, now in his mid-40s, had been at South American Gems Inc for just over a year after being internationally head hunted for the post of Chief Exploration &

Geological Officer. The firm had offered an attractive salary with benefits including a rent free six-bedroom country house in Chile, where Ned stayed for nine months before relocating to another rent-free house in Bogotá. A recently divorced Ned had jumped at the opportunity and quit his lecturing job in London.

"Sure," said Ned, replying to Boss's question. "This is Rosa Maria Gonzalez." Ned gestured to the lady on his right. "Rosa, this is John Bosman."

"And what a rose you are... absolutely enchanting," Boss said leaning across Ned, taking her hand and lightly kissing the back of it. As Boss leant across Ned with no regard whatsoever, he wreaked tobacco smoke. As Rosa spoke, Ned almost choked on the champagne as it was not quite what he expected.

Her reply was, "It's an honour to meet you too John Bosman."

Earlier, at the hotel, when Ned had awoken from his slumber and was getting ready for the event, Rosa was already dressed in a long velvet black dress with straps and a low back. She was an extremely attractive woman of 35 years with high cheekbones, and very smooth skin. She later confessed to having regular Botox injections to keep her skin in check. She had a shapely petite figure and the smallest waist that Ned had seen on anyone. As she sat in front of a dressing mirror, arranging her diamond jewellery and grooming her long dark silky hair, Ned compared her to his ex-wife Eva.

Ned met Eva aged 28 at an education convention when he was a senior lecturer in Geology at Imperial College London ten years previously. Eva was an Arts teacher at a secondary school in Highbury Park, London. After courting for almost a year they were married, and Ned arranged a mortgage on a house in Henley. Shortly after moving in, Eva gave up her teaching job to develop her creativeness, as she put it. Ned fully supported Eva's 'developing' career, he even arranged for an arts studio to be built as an extension to the house.

While Ned lectured at the college and took care of the mortgage, the household bills, arts material for Eva and her exhibition fees, Eva spent her days in the studio 'exploring her creativity'. Her art mainly consisted of hanging an inverted bucket of paint (in various colours) over a large flat canvas and watch it do its thing as the bucket moved across the canvas. That crisp newly built white studio looked like a scene from Armageddon within a month.

Five years after a relatively happy marriage, Eva's career finally began to take off as her art gained interest from overseas collectors. With things more settled and the future beginning to look bright, Ned and Eva decided to have children. Ned always dreamt of having a large family but that's when the problems began. Eva and Ned tried for years after, but it was not to be. Eventually an appointment at a fertility clinic revealed the problem lay with Ned and from that day on Eva would always remind him of that fact. That's when the raging arguments started and often ended in Ned storming out of the house in a drunken stupor.

Eight years after their marriage, a bitter divorce ensued and assets were split, including the house. Ned vowed from that day forward he would conceal any future wealth that he accumulated; he wasn't going to fall into that trap again. Over the following years, Ned had the odd relationship here and there but never wanted to marry again, that's until he met Rosa. Rosa was the woman he employed as a housekeeper when he relocated to the Bogotá residence after the previous housekeeper left to return to her family in Brazil. When he placed an advertisement in a newspaper, Rosa responded almost immediately.

She wasn't his housekeeper for long as they shortly started a relationship, who could resist a woman as perfect as Rosa, and she still insisted on keeping the house in order. Rosa was caring, quiet and totally devoted to Ned. She also made it clear from the start that she didn't want any children, which considering Ned was unable to provide, suited him fine. One day, she showed Ned her hysterectomy scars and an old crumpled photograph of a fair-haired child wrapped in a white blanket. The child couldn't have been more than a year old, Ned thought. When Rosa showed Ned the photograph, her exact words to him were 'baby girl die, Rosa too sad, no more children'.

When Ned questioned Rosa about the fairness of the child in contrast to Rosa's dark features, Rosa replied, "Father Americano, he go away."

Rosa spoke very little English, and if she did it was broken, at least that's what Ned thought. Raging arguments were non-existent. With Rosa, Ned felt he could get away with murder. He was looking forward to the future with her, even the idea of marriage had crossed his mind.

So now, back in the banqueting hall, Rosa's long worded unbroken response to Boss came as a shock to

Ned. He spoke again, "So, where have you been hiding this lovely lady?"

It was him again referring to Rosa. In his mind Ned thought 'away from you', so Ned diverted the question asking... "And John, yours?" indicating the young leggy busty blonde sat on the other side of Boss. Since they had taken their seats, she had been pampering herself in front of a handheld jewel encrusted cosmetic mirror whilst sipping glass after glass of champagne as they were delivered. On hearing Ned's voice, she immediately snapped the mirror shut and reached over Boss's belly.

She took Ned's hand and shook it firmly, her sharp red painted nails digging into his wrist. She also acknowledged Rosa with a wave. In a slurred American accent, she said, "Hiya, nice to meet ya both. I'm Linzi, Johns... Mr. Bosman's, um..." she threw a glance at Boss who was looking slightly uncomfortable, "personal assistant."

"Is that so?" Ned said, not at all shocked. "Well, I hope you last longer than the last one he had."

He jutted in, "Yes, Linzi's only been with us two weeks, I've been showing her the ins and outs of the business."

"I'm sure you have," Ned whispered under his breath.

Another waiter then approached the table carrying a large solid silver bowl with a ladle in it. He stopped behind Boss and Linzi. "Would the young lady care for some lobster bisque?" the waiter asked, he couldn't take his eyes off Linzi's ample cleavage and a long slender leg exposed from her thigh-high split red dress.

Linzi turned to face the waiter. "Lobster bish? What's that?" she slurred.

"It's a kind of soup my lovely," said Boss as his hand discreetly squeezed Linzi's exposed thigh.

"It doesn't have any big bulging lobster eyes floating in it, I hope," she joked, ringing her eyes and making them bulge.

"Certainly not," replied the waiter. "Just the meat of the lobster."

"Great," Linzi said lifting her soup bowl. "Fill it to the brim... and make sure I get loads of those big juicy lumpy bits. I could eat a horse."

Boss turned to Ned, inhaled on his cigar and said, "I do like a girl with a healthy appetite, wouldn't you agree Ned?" At that moment, a sudden wave of acid shot through Ned's gut.

Later, once Boss could see the other six people on the table were occupied with their lobster bisque, he shifted closer to Ned who was now opening a bottle of the red wine. As Ned was opening it, one could just decipher the band in the other room as they started to play a rendition of Black Betty by Ram Jam.

He spoke, "I've read that monthly report you emailed to my office last week. What a load of bull. It's just not good enough Ned."

Boss flicked his cigar ash into a solid silver ashtray. "Look, we've been mining at that Bogotá location for 3 months now, rigging ain't cheap you know. I don't pay you big bucks and give you a fancy house and car to tell me you've found nothing. This firm has had four highly successful mines, why should the one at Bogotá be any different? Our clients have high expectations, and I can't afford to let them down. I've seen the thermal images of that Bogotá mine, and they don't lie, I know those minerals are down there. I want them dug up, packed up and shipped to our clients by the end of the month."

Ned's report covered two mines. One in Chile, which he had been appointed to when he joined the firm, and a more recent mine in Bogotá. The Chile mine was proving to be quite successful, whereas the mine in Bogotá was losing money. Ned also had to report on locations that were possible exploration sites, this included a place called Greenstone Island. The island, mainly populated with green mossy rocks, was located in the Caribbean. Upon arriving at the island with its idyllic coves and sandy beaches, Ned fell in love with the place. He imagined living there with Rosa, building a place overlooking Turtle Bay. He had even discussed it with Rosa, who seemed keen on the idea. Her exact words were 'Sound nice. When go?' So, to throw Boss off track, Ned stated that the Island was a category NFIR (No Further Investigation Required). These categories did not get a look in. Further, in the description, Ned had written that the islanders' main occupation was fishing and were housed in corrugated iron shelters.

"As I wrote in the report John, it's not that easy. That Bogotá mine is deeper than what we thought and that comes with more complications. The miners are also leaving in their droves as they are concerned about their health and safety, and I am too. Many of them are getting serious lung conditions, so what little wages they get they have to spend on medical bills. We need to provide them with the proper safety equipment, it's essential." "I'm not wasting our money on petty stuff like that," Boss said.

"They should be grateful they have work, most of them are criminals anyway. If they want to leave, let them."

As he rambled on, Ned thought about Greenstone Island again. He remembered driving through the village where the buildings were no more than corrugated huts. At one place he passed, there was a makeshift doctor's sign and a long queue of local people, young and old, some women carrying sick babies.

Boss continued, "Just get some workers in from that Island you mentioned in the report, the one in the NFIR category with the mossy rocks. I'm sure they must be begging for work; they haven't got anything else better to do except sit around fishing all day. In fact, I'll discuss it with HR first thing in the morning and arrange a truck load to be sent to Bogotá. I'll also tell HR to have the cost of transport and living costs deducted from their wages. Remember Ned, I built this company from scratch, and I'm not letting any minor hitches bring it down. Either you get me some results soon with that mine in Bogotá, or you can say goodbye to your annual bonus."

Ned turned to Rosa who had hardly touched the soup and was sitting quietly with her hands in her lap. "Sorry my love, but I'm feeling a bit unwell, must be the lobster."

The rambling, the tobacco smoke, and unseasoned lobster had made Ned feel sick.

Rosa looked concerned, "You want water?" She retrieved a jug from the table.

Patting her on the arm, Ned reassured her, "No, no. I just need to go to the restroom for a minute. I'll be fine."

"You sure?"

"Don't worry my love, I'll be back soon."

Ned got up and walked off in the direction of the men's restroom grabbing a bottle of wine from another table on the way, much to the occupants' dismay. Little did he know, but the next time Ned was to see Rosa Marie Gonzalez was 15 years later.

The sound of Black Betty boomed through to the banqueting hall as the band in the other room turned up the volume. The song immediately drowned the music of the string quartet.

Boss stood up and banged his fist hard on the table, making the plates and cutlery shake. There's a sudden silence around all the tables in the hall. "Somebody shut those doors, I can't hear myself think!" A waiter immediately rushed to close the double doors which Ned had been looking through earlier. "And what idiot booked that band? I specifically said they were to have no music!" When he said they, he was referring to the back-office staff on the other side of the double doors.

"When I find out who it is, I want them sacked immediately, do you hear me?"

Beside him, Linzi sheepishly looked up from her near empty soup bowl.

Chapter 2

Next door to the men's restroom, the women's room was buzzing with excitement. An array of cosmetics and hair products covered the vanity shelf above the wash basins. Women were chatting as they meticulously applied makeup and styled their hair. Some scantily clothed women were sliding on short flower print dresses, others dressed in boob tubes, bell bottomed trousers and short miniskirts.

Holding Maggie's waist, Lola spun her around in front of a full-length mirror. "You can open your eyes now girl," she said to Maggie.

When Maggie opened her eyes, she didn't recognize the person in front of her. Gone was the turtleneck jumper, slacks and flat shoes which had become part of her daily office attire. In their place was a short strapless green dress which clung to every inch of her svelte figure.

The hem of the dress was high above her knees. 'How the Sisters at the orphanage would disapprove,' Maggie thought. Lola had helped Maggie choose the dress from a nearby department store during a lunch break. Maggie's usual tied back auburn hair had been released from its band and flowed around her bare shoulders. The thigh high white boots she wore, also a purchase from the store, made her feel so much taller, even though they only had a 3-inch heel. The boots were half a size too small and pinched her feet a bit, but Maggie liked them, and they were the only ones left in the store. Lola had applied Maggie's makeup, not too much, just enough to accentuate Maggie's natural fine bone structure and the green of her eyes. A pair of dangling green costume earrings and small pendant completed the look.

"I still think you should have gone for boots with a higher heel," Lola said from behind her.

"No these are perfect," Maggie said, admiringly turning one leg. She turned to face Lola who was dressed in a sparkling clingy black bodysuit with flared bottoms. Her dark Hispanic hair with a streak of burgundy red at the front, was styled in a bob, the sort where the fringe slopes across the forehead. She was constantly flicking it back to see clearly.

"You look great in that outfit too," she said to Lola.

They gave each other a long bear hug.

Maggie continued, "You're such a good friend. I couldn't have done this without you."

"Ah, it's nothing," Lola said, flicking back her hair. "It's about time you let your hair down and enjoy a night out. You spend too many evenings cooped up in that dingy apartment."

Lola had been the only real friend Maggie had met when she joined South America Gems Inc. a year ago when she was 19. She had been disowned by her parents and found herself homeless until a hostel in Caracas took her in. Lola never discussed why they disowned her, and Maggie never brought the subject up.

The two got on like a house on fire, even though they had opposite personalities. Lola was the rebellious type and told stories about where she had been, crazy people she had met, and the scrapes she had gotten into. This fascinated Maggie. The orphanage had been so strict, and at this point in time she wanted to be more like Lola. They got on so well that they decided to rent an apartment together. With them both working, it wasn't long before they had saved enough money for a deposit. Lola even gave up cigarettes. They rented a cheap two bedroomed apartment, a bus ride away from the office. It was perfect for them. A few weeks after moving into the apartment, Lola was back on the cigarettes much to Maggie's annoyance, as she hated the smell of cigarette smoke, and the apartment began to stink of it.

Back in the women's restroom Lola sprayed them both with a bottle of Eau de toilette that she found on the vanity shelf. They then linked arms with Lola vowing "And my next mission is to find you a man." Maggie nodded in agreement.

"Then let's go girl!" And off they went to join the office party.

Chapter 3

Other women from the typing pool were gathered in front of a long buffet counter deciding what food to choose from the limited selection of tapas, cold meats, olives and sandwiches. Maggie placed some slices of chorizo and a couple of cheese sandwiches on her plastic plate, and picked up a cup containing orange juice, served to her by a tall young man standing at the other end of the buffet counter.

Lola was already drinking from her cup, the house white wine, whilst smoking a cigarette. "This wine is disgusting," she said and pointed her cup towards the closed double doors. "I bet they're not drinking this trash on the other side."

"It's a shame Carlos couldn't make it," lied Maggie. "Nah, it's not his thing," Lola said, taking a long drag on her cigarette and puffing small smoke rings. "Besides, I want to have some fun girl, we haven't been out together in ages."

Carlos was Lola's Latino boyfriend. She met him two months after they moved into the apartment. Lola would always drag Maggie out on a Friday night, the one night of the week that Maggie would go out. The bar was conveniently situated near the apartment, a short walk away.

Lola was always checking out the talent as she

called it, and on Friday nights the bar was packed. Lola was always the popular one with the men. They hardly approached Maggie, and if they did, she would shy away from their drunken banter. She often sat alone, drinking coke, dressed in her turtleneck jumper and slacks as Lola busied herself flirting with the men. Lola would often bring a man back to the apartment, a different one every week, and she was getting quite a reputation at that bar.

The first time Maggie met Carlos was in the kitchen of their apartment one morning. Maggie had walked in looking for her apartment keys, and there Carlos was with just a towel tied around his midriff helping himself to juice straight from the carton.

Carlos was different to the other men Lola brought home, as she saw this one again...and again. Since their encounter in the kitchen, Carlos was always around the apartment plonking himself on the couch in the living room to watch baseball whilst smoking joints. Lola would often join him on the couch and take a few puffs too. Eventually, Maggie and Lola stopped going to the bar. There was no point, Carlos was the only man Lola was interested in. Maggie started to stay in her bedroom whenever he came over, reading magazines. She didn't like him at all. Often, she would hear them arguing, mainly about Carlos' job status, which was non-existent. He would always be shouting, "Tomorrow, tomorrow."

One day, when Carlos wasn't there, Maggie told Lola that he was a bad influence on her, but she wouldn't listen. Carlos was the best thing that had ever happened to her. She was smitten.

At the office party, sipping her orange juice, Maggie

knew full well that Carlos was at the apartment, watching baseball with his mates. The apartment was going to stink of pot when they got home.

As the band started playing a rendition of We are the Champions by Queen, Felipe from the administration department strutted over to them. He was dressed in a tight-fitting salmon pink suit, pink shirt and a thin black tie. He had a yellow carnation pinned to his lapel.

"Hello my darlings, and how are my two favourite people in the world?" He grabbed Maggie by her arm admiringly looked her up and down. "Oh my god, you look absolutely fabulous my darling."

"Thanks Felipe," said Maggie, "You're so kind.... it's all Lola's work."

Felipe turned to face Lola. "Is that so?" as he lightly touched her arm. "Well next time I need a stylist, you will definitely be first on my list."

He looked at the collection of food on the buffet counter and tutted, "They really know how to push the boat out, don't they? Anyway, I thought I'd come over and cheer you both up as you were looking so bored. I think it's about time we got this party started." Out of nowhere he held up a magnum bottle of Dom Perignon. He grabbed two empty cups from the table and filled them up. "One for you my darling," handing it to Maggie. "And... one for you Lola, equally as lovely."

"How did you manage to get hold of that?" asked Lola, taking the bottle from him and scrutinizing the label. "Let's just say that I have made some very good connections." Felipe sneaked a look back at the tall man at the far end of the buffet counter who in turn gave him an affirming nod. "Anyway, enjoy my darlings, must dash, I have a pressing engagement, if you know what I mean?" Felipe said winking.

With a flick of his foot he headed in the direction of the tall man, shouting back, "And I'll see you two on the dance floor later giving it your thang." He then proceeded to wiggle his bum and waved his arms in the air singing along to the music. "We are the Champions of the World."

Maggie and Lola collapsed into a fit of giggles.

Chapter 4

"Ladies and Gentlemen," the lead vocalist of the band spoke at the front of a raised stage. "We'd like to thank you all for your hospitality tonight. I would like to take this opportunity to introduce you to the members of our band, 'Dare to Dream'."

Each one of the four men in the band had long unruly hair, and wore a faded t-shirt tucked into very tight bell bottom denims. The lead vocalist continued, "On lead guitar we have Aiden." Aiden strummed a few chords on his guitar and the gathered crowd below the stage cheered. "On base we have Levi." Levi strummed a few chords and the crowd cheered again. "And on drums we have the very talented Jack, a.k.a 'Woody.'" A man with long dark hair gave it all he had on the drums, and cymbals and there was an even louder cheer from the crowd. "And finally, there's my good self, Ethan, lead vocalist." Another loud cheer. "Well ladies and gentlemen, we'd like to play a song which is close to our hearts. We spend months on the road, so we dedicate this song to our families back home whom we miss. I hope you enjoy it and feel free to sing along... and remember... dare to dream." He gave a signal to the members of the band and started counting 1,2,3. The song was Sweet Home Alabama. The office crowd let out a huge cheer and started dancing and singing along.

As they played the song, Jack thought about his

family in Alabama. There lived his mother Grace, his father Frank, and two older brothers David and Glen. The family farm was located on acres of land surrounded by a thick forest. As Jack hit the drums, he thought back to the days as a young boy when, with his brothers, helped to muck out the animal sheds and build wire fences with his father.

He also thought about those long hot summer days when there was no school and he would help his father collect wood from the forest. While his father used a circular saw to construct another piece of furniture for the house, Jack would sit on a tree stump and attempt to carve wooden spoons from the scraps of wood he found. Jack's father always had his sleeves rolled up. He was always busy making something out of wood if he wasn't working on the farm. He even built the boys a treehouse deep in the forest.

Jack also thought about the first time he hit a drum. Jack's parents bought him a toy drum on his fifth birthday. He banged on that drum so hard all day, every day for a week, that it fell apart. His parents decided not to buy another one, but Jack never forgot about that first toy drum.

After school finished, Jack got a job in a local supermarket for a few hours every day when he wasn't helping at the farm. When he had saved enough money, he bought his first proper drum kit. That was eight years ago when he was sixteen. It was in the treehouse in the forest. After work and his chores, Jack would take a portable radio, listen to popular music of the time, and practise his drumming skills.

His brothers, being older than Jack, stopped playing in the treehouse, so Jack had it all to himself. He could bang those drums so hard in the forest, no one could hear for miles. He soon acquired the nickname Woody from those that knew him, and it stuck with him ever since. Later, he joined a local band that was advertising for a drummer. The whole band would practise together in the treehouse, stopping occasionally just to eat freshly baked cookies provided by Jack's mother.

As the years went on, Jack's farm duties became less and less and his brothers, now grown men, were practically running the farm. Seeing that the farm was being taken care of, Jack told his parents that the band had decided to hit the road and they gave him their blessing.

Now, aged twenty-four and nearly four years on the road, Jack missed home, but he loved playing in the band and travelling from region to region throughout North and South America.

At every stop, he would call his family and they would each talk for ages; him about the band and the places he had been, them about the farm. His father would say, "I've still got all those wooden spoons that you made." And they would both have a laugh about that.

Jack also made a point of making it back to the farm every year for Thanksgiving. The band mainly played in small clubs and bars and were occasionally booked for office parties. They always had a warm welcome wherever they went. Playing drums was Jack's passion in life, that was until later in the evening, when he first laid eyes on Maggie.

Chapter 5

Later in the evening, the band was playing Do You Think I'm Sexy by Rod Stewart. Lola and Maggie were now standing at the far end of a packed dance floor, mainly consisting of the back-office staff.

"Look," said Lola, as she pointed to a familiar figure on the dance floor. "It's Ned from the other side."

"Who's that he's dancing with?" Maggie asked.

In the middle of the dance floor, Ned was dancing with a woman dressed in a long slinky red dress. He had a bottle of red wine in one hand which he would occasionally take a swig out of. His black jacket was hanging off his shoulders and his bow tie tilted to one side. He was attempting to dance in circles around the woman singing, "Do You Think I'm Sexy?" at the top of his voice.

The woman towered above him in red stiletto shoes. She had her arms in the air, one holding a glass of champagne, her slender body moving in time to the music. "That's the new girl Linzi," Lola shouted above the sound of the music. "Boss's personal assistant, apparently... Must be on a good wage to afford a dress like that. Recently, I was in a meeting with him and some guys from marketing. I was taking notes and I heard Boss say that she will be a great asset to the firm. If you ask me, the only assets he's interested in is squeezed into that tight dress." She threw a look at Maggie. They then spotted Felipe beckoning

Maggie and Lola to join him and a group of others on the dance floor.

"Come on Maggie, let's show them how to do it."

Lola took hold of Maggie's arm and pulled her onto the dance floor where they danced to song after song of popular 70s hits.

Much later in the evening, the band was playing a rendition of Burning Love by Elvis. A single bead of sweat trickled down the side of Maggie's hot rosy cheeks, her long auburn hair flowing wildly around her face. The champagne made her forget about the pain in her feet where the boots were pinching.

Eyes closed, she danced to the music feeling every beat fill her body. Little did she realise that she had blind danced away from the group, away from Lola and Felipe. She only opened her eyes when a sharp pain caught the side of her ribs. She had reached the front of the stage and as she looked up a pair of mesmerizing blue eyes were staring right at her. Jack's eyes.

Chapter 6

Fifteen years and three children later, Maggie still maintained the same figure that she had at the office party. Her long hair was tied back, and she was hanging up washing in the garden of a modest detached country house with white timber slats. At the end of the garden was a river where a boat called the Flying Fish was moored to a jetty. It was a hot summer's day in July and her son Sam, aged twelve, was entertaining his eighteen-month-old twin sisters, Beth and Alice, as they played in a round shallow paddling pool. Sam's hair was dark brown and wavy in contrast to the twins' blonde locks. He was throwing a large red beach ball at them as they sat in the pool. The twins tried to catch it but kept failing and fell about giggling. Every time they missed it, Sam retrieved the ball from the garden and threw it at them again.

A blue car pulled up in front of the house next to a parked station wagon. Maggie turned to look and see who it was and waved as her best friend Martha emerged from the car with her husband Dan. Martha carried a small baby in her arms wrapped in a pink blanket. Their son Tod age twelve, who was Sam's best friend emerged from the back door of the car. He was playing on a small gadget in his hands and didn't look up. The Taylor family were Jack and Maggie's nearest American neighbours living a few miles away. Since moving to the house just before Sam was born, situated near the town of San Pengio, a small port on the north coast of Venezuela, they had built up a strong friendship. Maggie was happy to see them all as they didn't get many visitors to the house, and she was especially keen to see the new baby. She dropped her washing basket and rushed over to greet them.

"Oh, isn't she gorgeous," said Maggie, as Martha pulled back the blanket to reveal the baby's tiny face. "I'll just get the twins and put the kettle on. Go on in, the door is open."

As Dan and Martha walked towards the front door of the house, Martha said, "Isn't your phone working Maggie, we tried calling you to let you know we were coming but the line wasn't working."

"Oh, not again. We keep having problems with that line. It's because we live so far out. I'll ask Jack to check it out when he comes home."

Tod, still with his head down, engaged with the gadget, walked slowly towards Sam. Sam with the red ball clutched to his chest, watched Tod as he walked towards him. Sam was curious to know what he was playing with.

Tod stopped in front of Sam. "What's that?" asked Sam, looking at the gadget in Tod's hands.

Tod looked up to Sam. "It's called a Gameboy. Want to have a go?"

"You bet!" Sam immediately threw the red ball hard past Maggie, who was drying off the twins. The ball bounced on the jetty and landed on the deck of the Flying Fish.

Dan and Martha stayed in the kitchen where Maggie was feeding the twins vegetable puree, it was all baby talk.

Sam and Tod stayed in the garden taking turns playing on the Gameboy.

The Taylors stayed for just over an hour and when they went home Maggie remained in the kitchen with the twins in their highchairs, preparing lunch, as Jack would be back from the shop soon. Sam felt alone and bored after Tod had gone home, and it was only the first week of the school vacation. There wasn't much to do for a young boy stuck in the middle of nowhere except play with the twins, watch TV or ride his bike around the neighbourhood. Sam walked into the front room, picked up a pack of cards and the TV remote from a shelf.

He sat down crossed legged on the floor and began laying out the cards to play Patience, a game his dad had taught him. He pressed a button on the remote control and the TV came on. There was a young ballerina dressed in a pale blue outfit, she must have been about 10 years old. She was being taught certain moves and poses by her dance instructor, some involved standing on the tips of her toes.

Sam stood up, put his arms above his head, and tried to stand on his toes, but the pain was excruciating and collapsed down to the floor. Defeated, he flicked to another channel. An old black and white film was on. Two men with feathers in their hats were sword fighting. Sam jumped up again and mimicked fighting with a sword complete with all the sounds.

When he was tired of doing that he flicked to another channel and another film. A man was tied up in a chair, his feet and hands bound, and he had brown tape over his mouth. Another man with a black trilby hat on and dressed in a white suit had one leg up, resting on a table next to the tied-up man. The man in the trilby hat had a gun in one hand and a handset to a phone in the other.

In a mean Italian accent, he said, "Bring me the money tomorrow or for your brother there will be no tomorrow."

Sam pursed his lips tight as though taped across like the other man, put his wrists together and tried to say, "Help... help... somebody free me." But it just came out like mumbo jumbo. Sam flicked the channel again.

This time, the mainline news was on. At the bottom of the screen was a scrolling weather ticker. Behind the female news reporter Sam was drawn to a street artist juggling batons.

Sam jumped up and retrieved three green apples from a fruit bowl and tried to copy the juggler, but he kept dropping them. He watched the juggler on the screen and tried to follow his method again.

He was annoyed when the camera panned down to the face of a Latin American man and the juggler was suddenly out of view. The camera zoomed out and it was apparent to Sam that the man on TV had no legs.

He was sitting in a wheelchair with a woman behind him holding the handles. Sam, now exhausted, sat down, and watched the man with no legs as the reporter said, "We will now speak to Jose Fernandez who has a remarkable story to tell."

A microphone appeared in front of the man as the reporter said, "When you are ready, Mr. Fernandez, in your own words."

The man was eager to tell his story. "Yes, it's a miracle, a miracle from God." as he looked up to the sky. "I still can't believe it. I was working in a field in Colombia about 2 years ago now, when the old landmine blew up. It took both my legs straight off. I remember this now. A week later I woke up in the hospital in Cartagena. The doctors say my family is around me. I look around at all these people by my bed. I don't know anyone. I don't even know who I am."

The man started to cry. The news reporter handed him a tissue and he composed himself. "These people take me home. For 2 years I don't know who I'm living with, I can't remember anything. I don't know my wife," he indicated his wife standing behind him. "My mother, my father, my sisters, my brothers no-one," he cried again. "The doctors said I got metal stuck in my head when that bomb went off and they couldn't take it out, too dangerous. That bomb not only took my legs which I can deal with, but took my life memories too," crying more.

The camera panned back to the reporter. "We have spoken to the medical staff at Cartagena General and they have verified Mr. Fernandez's former condition to be true. Then what happened Mr. Fernandez, take your time?" The reporter beckoned the camera man to come closer to him.

"Well, yesterday I was sitting in my rocking chair on the veranda of the house as I do every evening, wishing I could remember something, anything. I felt so down, I even thought about ending it all. I felt trapped in a body that I didn't know. The sun was just going down, and then I saw it."

"Saw what Mr. Fernandez?"

He looked up to the reporter. "A butterfly. A beautiful blue butterfly. It was the most beautiful butterfly I had ever seen in my life. I watched it as it flew around me for a while, then it landed right here on my hand.

He pointed to a spot on the back of his hand where he had a small angel tattoo. "As soon as it landed, I felt this kind of force through my body, a feeling I can't explain. I think God touched me that evening."

"Then what happened Mr. Fernandez?"

"It was only on the back of my hand a few seconds, then it flew away," he sobbed again. "Then from nowhere, it came back just like that."

"What, the butterfly?" asked the reporter.

"No... my memory came back. I remember everyone and everything. I got my life back."

Suddenly several other faces appeared behind him and next to him smiling, holding crosses to the sky and praising God, his whole family.

The camera went back to the presenter. "Well, what an amazing story. Thank you for sharing it with us Mr. Fernandez. What's even more amazing is the medical staff treating Mr. Fernandez have confirmed that a brain scan performed shortly after the incident showed no sign of the pre-existing metal whatsoever."

"Sam!" It was Maggie calling from the kitchen. "Your father's home and lunch is ready."

Sam switched the TV off and jumped up high into a cross shape simultaneously shouting, "Ker boom!" He exited the room leaving the apples and cards scattered all over the floor.

Chapter 7

In the middle of the kitchen was a long wooden table. A freshly baked loaf of bread was in the centre along with a large bowl of chicken salad. Maggie was busy cleaning up the mucky twins who had just been fed. Sam's father Jack, wearing a chequered shirt, was already sitting at the table scribbling on a glossy leaflet.

At thirty-nine Jack still maintained his good looks. His previous long dark hair dark was now much shorter and had a couple of streaks of grey in it. Once the band had finished their tour around Caracas with Maggie by his side when she wasn't working at the firm, Jack packed his drum kit away and got a job as a salesman in a furniture shop.

Eight months after meeting at the office party they were married at a registry office in Caracas with only two nuns from Maggie's orphanage as witnesses. Lola had left Caracas by this time and had moved to Nicaragua with Carlos. Maggie and Lola's friendship had drifted apart, and she didn't even have her new address or phone number.

Jack and Maggie lived in an apartment for a while until they had saved enough money for the deposit on this house near San Pengio. Jack also had some extra money he saved from the band and was able to get a lease on a small shop 5 miles away in town where he sold the furniture that he had started to make since moving into the house. Watching his father in those early years had come in handy. Making furniture also kept Jack's body in good shape. The shop provided the family with a modest income, enough to get by for a family of five. The people in town preferred to shop at Ripley's superstore where they sold furniture in bulk and a lot lower than Jack's prices.

As Sam walked into the kitchen, he saw Jack scribbling on the leaflet with a pen and said.

"Dad, can I have a Gameboy?"

Jack looked up from the glossy leaflet and said,

"What's that son?"

"Sam, go over to the sink and wash your hands please," demanded Maggie. Sam obediently walked over to the sink where he spotted some claws sticking out of a crumpled piece of newspaper on the side. He washed his hands and dried them constantly staring at the menacing claws.

"The Taylors dropped by today," Maggie said, talking to Jack. "You should have seen the baby, Jack, she's gorgeous. They haven't got a name for her yet, but I suggested Mary Anne, what do you think?"

Jack continued to look at the leaflet pondering. "Yeh, that's nice."

Sam approached the twins with his hands behind his back and suddenly dangled a dead crab in front of them, opening and closing the claws. The twins started to cry. "Sam!" Maggie shouted. "Put that back, sit down and eat your food."

Sam threw it back on to the newspaper and sat at the table grabbing a knife to cut the loaf.

"You really shouldn't have bought so much crab Jack, I don't know what to do with it all."

"I couldn't resist it; it was a bargain and I know how much you like bargains. Just freeze it hun. A guy was selling it at the market this morning, you should have seen the queue, everyone wanted some. Talking about bargains, I picked this up too." Jack started to wave the leaflet in the air and pointed to a small advert on the front which he had ringed with a pen that said, 'Bargain Evergreens only

$20 a log & Free Shipping.' "This Evergreen would make some great mahogany pieces."

Maggie approached Jack smoothing down her apron. She took the colourful leaflet. Across the top it said, 'Greenstone Island, an idyllic island set in the Caribbean Sea.' There was a map of the island on the front showing colourful pictures of the lagoon, the forest, the sandy bays, the fishing harbour and a village. She unfolded the leaflet which displayed photographs of newly built villas all with pools located in the north of the island. Each had an expensive sale price next to it. Sadly, she handed the leaflet back to Jack.

"Anyway, I'm thinking of taking the Flying Fish out there this afternoon, I haven't taken her out in months. Mateo, Jack's Hispanic shop assistant said he doesn't mind looking after the shop this afternoon. I might even buy a few logs if they're good quality and have them shipped back."

Sam, who had sandwiched some of the chicken from the salad bowl into the dry bread perked up, "Can I come, Dad?"

"Is up to your mother," Jack said as he looked towards

Maggie who had a concerned look on her face. "Are you sure that's a good idea Jack?"

"He'll be fine, I'll take good care of him," Jack reassured Maggie. "He's old enough now."

"Ok, but don't forget he's going swimming tomorrow morning with Tod, so you can't be too late coming back, he needs an early night."

"Don't worry hun," Jack looked at the clock on the wall. "If we go soon, we should be back by eight." Jack then looked out of the window. There was a breeze through the trees and the sky was clear blue. "Looks like it's gonna be a great afternoon for sailing, son."

Sam's was so excited he quickly devoured the chicken sandwich. He wanted to go as soon as possible.

After lunch, Jack was with Maggie by the front door. She had the twins either side of her holding her hands. Jack had a small rucksack over his back with some sandwiches and drink that Maggie packed. Sam was already eagerly walking towards the boat, with the pack of playing cards in his hand.

Jack called out to him, "Aren't you going to say goodbye to your mother and sisters?"

Sam reluctantly walked back and kissed Maggie quickly on the cheek. "Bye Mum." He then pulled a face at the twins who both giggled. "Bye Beth, bye Alice," and Sam walked off again.

Jack bent down and told the twins to be good for their mother and gave them each a small peck on the cheek. He then stood up and further reassured Maggie that Sam will be fine in his care. He then gave her a kiss and said, "I love you Maggie"

"I love you too Jack." As Jack turned to follow Sam, Maggie shouted, "Make sure Sam wears a life jacket."

Jack waved back at her, "I'll make sure of it hun."

Maggie went back indoors with the twins. In the kitchen she wandered over to a calendar on the wall. She flipped it over to August and wrote in one of the spaces on a particular date. 'Jack and Maggie's wedding anniversary'. She gazed at the entry for a while thinking about a present for Jack. She took her apron off, retrieved her purse from a drawer, gathered the twins and grabbed the keys to the station wagon. As she left the house to drive to Ripley's stores, she failed to notice that Jack had left the leaflet and his wallet on the table. She also had forgotten to tell Jack about the faulty phone.

Chapter 8

Jack was at the helm of the boat steering. Sam stood next to him, wearing a life jacket. Jack was showing Sam how the boat operated, what all the various dials and levers meant. Sam was eager to learn. They soon reached the open sea, which was calm with just a few waves. Jack let Sam have a go on the boat's steering wheel from time to time, he was very happy. As they hit a wave, the red beach ball which Sam had thrown earlier that day, rolled across the deck and hit Jack on the foot.

"Have the twins been playing on the boat again?" asked Jack.

"I don't know," Sam sheepishly replied.

"The number of times I've told Maggie that they're not allowed on the boat!"

Sam remained silent.

Jack noticed that the wind was beginning to pick up. "Want to do some proper sailing son?"

"Awesome," said Sam smiling. "Then let's put the sails up."

Jack switched the engine off and proceeded to put the sails up. While he was doing that Sam looked at the colourful fishes which were circling the boat. Once the sails were up, the Flying Fish looked glorious as she sailed the Caribbean Sea towards Greenstone Island.

As they sailed, Jack chatted to Sam about his time in

the band when he was known as Woody and the different places he'd been to before he met Maggie. He talked about his childhood years spent on the farm, about the treehouse and the toy drum. At the end of their chat, Jack put his arm around Sam's shoulder and said, "I will always be there for you, Maggie and the twins, we're family."

After a couple of hours of sailing, the sky began to darken, and it started to patter with rain. As Jack took the sails down, he thought about the evergreen logs and how many he might buy. He felt in his back pocket for the leaflet where he made a note of the quantity and felt for his wallet. He then felt the other pocket and went down into the cabin and searched through the rucksack. He couldn't find the leaflet or the wallet anywhere.

"Dammit, I must have left them back at the house," Jack said to himself as he went back on deck.

"Sam, have you seen my wallet?"

"No, not seen it," said Sam. "Is that why they called you Woody? Because you forget things," he laughed.

"Very funny son... we'll have to turn back, there's no point. I'll take you to the island another time, I promise." Sam was disappointed, he was really looking forward to having a little adventure on the island, something to tell Tod about.

When Jack was searching for the wallet in the rucksack, he saw there was a message on his mobile phone, so he went back into the cabin to retrieve it. Neither Jack nor Sam had heard the phone ring earlier.

The message from Maggie was about how she had come home from shopping and found his wallet and leaflet on the table. She also said she was calling from Martha's house as the home phone wasn't working. Jack called the number back. Dan picked it up saying that Maggie had called a repair man, and he should be getting to the house about seven. Jack looked at the small clock in the cabin. It was six thirty, so he decided to try and call her later.

By the time the boat got back on the river it was very dark and pelting with rain. There was occasional thunder and lightning. Jack was at the helm wearing a black waterproof jacket he found in the cabin. The hood on the jacket was up, covering most of his face. Sam was inside the small cabin keeping dry. He was eating some of the sandwiches that Maggie had made earlier and trying to build a tower with the pack of cards. As the boat rocked back and forth the tower kept falling. He got up to peer out of a steamed up porthole to look at the impressive bolts of lightning and his vision was drawn to a hunched dark shape across the bank of the river looking straight at the boat as it went by.

Half an hour later, Jack turned the engine off, left the keys in the ignition and tied the boat to its mooring spot outside the house. He looked towards the house and a telephone repair van was just leaving.

Sam was building one final tower and he placed the last card on the top. He finally done it and waved his arms in the air, proud of his accomplishment. "Sam, we're home," Jack shouted from the jetty. "Can you bring the rucksack?"

As Jack dialled the home phone, he saw the red ball rolling on the deck and jumped on to retrieve it. Suddenly a long bolt of lightning traversed the night sky, a few seconds after that the thunder made a tremendous sound.

A loose mast on the boat fell out of place, and as Maggie answered the phone, there was a huge gust of wind and the mast swung with full force into Jack's head as he straightened up, knocking him into the river which now had a strong current. The heavy gust of wind also caused the boat to jolt to one side and Sam's tower of cards fell flat on the table.

Disappointed, Sam packed the cards up and ascended the stairs from the cabin with the rucksack. Taking off his life jacket he said, "Dad, did you hear that thunder, it was awesome?"

Sam searched around the deck, but Jack was nowhere to be seen. Sam looked towards the house and concluded, 'Dad must have been in a real hurry to see Mum'.

Jack's mobile phone was carried along by the river's current. There was no sign of Jack. As it slowly sank, Maggie's voice can be heard saying, "Jack... Jack... are you there?"

Chapter 9

A month later, after a long search of the river there was no sign of Jack. Jack was a good swimmer, and it was assumed that he had been hit when the bolt of lightning struck.

A memorial service was held by the river. A large crowd had gathered all dressed in black. Martha was comforting Maggie who was sobbing uncontrollably. Tod was also there with Dan holding the baby. Sam was standing solemn holding the twins' hands who didn't really understand what was going on.

All of Jack's family were there too, as well as Mateo from the shop. He had kept it going for the last month, but the stock was rapidly declining. Two nuns from the orphanage, who were witnesses at Jack and Maggie's wedding, were also there. A local preacher was giving a sermon.

At the end of the sermon, Jack's father Frank, threw a wooden spoon into the river, he was inconsolable. Sam decided he couldn't take it anymore. He let go of the twin's hands and weaved his way out of the crowd. Maggie called out for him, but he continued and ran along the riverbank to the place where the boat was still moored.

Sam, sobbing, threw himself at the side of the boat and thumped it with all his might as he shouted, "Come back Dad, come back. You're not dead, you're not."

Chapter 10

Two weeks after the sermon, a man was erecting a 'For Sale' sign outside the house. A taxi pulled up at the front and a man dressed in a blue jacket with brass buttons, cream shirt and white trousers got out. He paid the taxi driver, who drove off. Maggie was sitting in an armchair in the living room.

It was the day of what should have been their wedding anniversary. She was holding a framed wedding photograph of herself and Jack to her chest. Beside her, on a shelf was Jack's wallet and a small white unopened box with the name of the store Ripley's on it.

Maggie liked the scent of the wallet, as it reminded her of Jack. Sam was sitting on the floor watching the twins play with some plastic toy bricks. He hardly played with them anymore.

"Why don't you go and see Tod, he would be pleased to see you? You could play with that game he brought last time?" Maggie said to Sam.

"Don't want to, I want to stay here with you, Beth and Alice."

Maggie only came out of her trance like state when the front doorbell rang. "It's probably that man that rang earlier about Dad's boat."

Sam said as he got up and headed towards the netted window. Earlier that day a man had spoken to Sam briefly about coming to the house to see the boat. He had asked to speak to his father, but Sam said that no one was there but his mum would be back soon. She was out grocery shopping with the twins at the time. The doorbell rang again, a longer, more persistent ring.

Maggie flinched. She put the frame back on the shelf face down and smoothed out her creased dress. She walked to the front door, obtaining the Flying Fish keys from a hook in the hallway. Sam discreetly pulled the net curtains back and observed an old man with white hair and a trimmed white beard fiddling with a red cravat around his neck. He wore a sailor's cap and was carrying a small white plastic bag. There was something about this man that triggered Sam's memory. Maggie opened the door slowly and the man lifted his cap.

"Good after..." the man paused. "Maggie?"

Maggie moved away from the glare of the sun that blocked the man's face. She looked more closely at the man wondering how he knew her. With a look of disbelief, she said, "No, it can't be, can it... Ned?"

Sam watched through the window as Maggie then closed the door behind her, and the two walked towards the boat deep in conversation. As they went, Sam had a flashback to the night of the tragedy, the night when he was looking out of the porthole. When the lightning struck, Sam saw flashes of the white beard and the red cravat on the dark hunched shape on the riverbank. He was sure that the person on the bank that night, was this man, walking down to the boat.

As Ned was looking around the boat with great admiration, he noticed that a mast had come out of place and clicked it back into position. Whilst he was holding onto the post, he turned to Maggie who was also standing on the deck.

"She's a beautiful boat Maggie, your husband must be so proud. I can't understand why he would want to sell her. When do you think he can provide me with the papers to sign?"

"Oh, you can sign the papers now, Ned. You see, my husband Jack was cruelly taken from us," she hesitated. "He was hit by a bolt of lightning."

Ned looked shocked. "Oh, that's awful, I'm so sorry to hear that Maggie," he said, as he held his cap to his chest as a mark of respect.

Chapter 11

Ned and Maggie returned to the house. The man erecting the 'For Sale' sign had left. Maggie led Ned into the kitchen, and she prepared some coffee. Sam had left the living room door ajar so that he could hear everything the man was saying.

After Ned signed the papers, he took an envelope packed with hundred dollar notes out of his white plastic bag and handed it to Maggie. She took it and left it on the table. She didn't need to check it; she could trust Ned. She gave him the keys to the boat as she said. "So, what happened, I presume you left the firm as I didn't see you come to the typing department after that party?"

"Yes, I left in... what year was it now... oh yes... 1978. I just had enough of the firm's politics and the way they operated. Anyway, I had no family ties, so I sold some shares that I accumulated over the years and my flat in London and bought a sailing boat. I sailed around the Caribbean for a while, stopping for months at a time at the different islands. Eventually I settled at a place called Greenstone Island, got myself a nice little place at Turtle Bay. I just do a bit of fishing from time to time, you know, I lead a simple life now. I still do the odd bit of sailing, just around Greenstone, but my boat is old and withered now and needs replacing... a bit like me." They both laughed, it was nice to see a smile on Maggie's face. "I've been looking for a new boat for a while, that's when I saw the card advertising the Flying Fish."

"Oh, I've heard of that place, Greenstone Island," said Maggie. "Jack, my husband, mentioned it once."

"And you Maggie, when did you leave the firm?"

"Oh, I left soon after I met Jack, so the same year as you. You remember my friend Lola, don't you?"

"How could I forget."

"Well, she was sacked as she was caught smoking an illegal substance in the ladies restroom one day and that was that. We moved from the apartment we shared, and I rented a place with Jack. She left town with her boyfriend Carlos to go to Nicaragua, I never heard from her again."

"Carlos?"

"Yes, that's right, did you know him?" "The name rings a bell."

As Maggie was speaking, Ned thought back to a news bulletin he saw recently. He often watched a TV channel dedicated to mining. Anyone connected to mining could be mentioned on that channel, even if they worked in the mail room. Ned made sure no one knew where he was going when he left the firm to go sailing.

There was even news about John Bosman on that channel, but whenever his name was mentioned, Ned quickly switched the TV off. He didn't want that grinning face ruining his idyllic existence. Anyway, on this one particular bulletin there were a couple of mugshots. At the time, Ned thought he knew the woman, but he wasn't sure. He remembered the man's name was Carlos something or other, a man wanted for drug trafficking and various other crimes in Nicaragua. There was also a mugshot of his wife. A woman who looked a lot older than her 35 years. After putting two and two together, Ned realized that it must have been Lola.

Just then, Sam entered the kitchen with the twins clinging on to his top walking behind him. He wanted an excuse to have a good look at this man. Maggie was by the kitchen counter preparing some drinks for Sam and the twins. Ned was drinking from his mug of coffee.

"Mum," said Sam looking over at the pile of money spilling out from the envelope on the table. "You left this in the other room."

Maggie turned and took the small white box from Sam. Ned saw that it has 'Ripley's' written on the side. "Thanks Sam, that's the watch I bought for Jack. He won't be needing it now. I'll ask Dan if he wants it."

As Maggie put the box away in a cupboard, Ned sensed her sadness. Sam then spotted the Greenstone Island leaflet on the side sticking out of some other papers. It was the leaflet Jack was scribbling on the day of the tragedy. As he went to pick up the leaflet, one of the twins turned around to look at the strange man in their kitchen. She looked at his wrinkly hands holding his mug. Ned looked up from his mug at the twin and nearly fell out of his chair spilling his coffee. Concerned, Maggie, rushed over to him.

"Are you alright Ned?"

Ned composed himself. "Just had a funny turn, that's all, I'll be ok."

"I'll fetch some water. Sam can you take the twins back to the other room. I'll bring some drinks in soon."

Sam, with the leaflet in his hand, twins by his heels

walked back past the white bearded man in the red cravat taking a good look. Ned raised his cap to them and smiled. Once they had gone back into the other room, Maggie filled a glass with water and handed it to Ned. As Ned thanked Maggie, he took the opportunity to look closely at her face. It was the first time he has ever noticed that she had green eyes and a small dark mole on her chin, no bigger than a pin prick.

Later, Maggie and Ned were standing at the front door.

"Well Maggie, take good care of yourself. It was great to see you again after all this time. Feel free to come and visit me at Turtle Bay, with your family and I'll rustle us up a little fish dish. There's a ferry that runs to the Island four times a day from the port at San Pengio."

"I'll see Ned, but I'm not sure where we will be living once the house and the business are sold."

"Oh well, you are all always welcome to pop on by as they say in England. I hope everything works out for you and your family and I promise I'll take good care of the Flying Fish."

"I'm sure you will Ned."

Ned waved back at her with his cap as he headed toward the boat jangling the keys as he went. As he was leaving, Maggie wondered how he knew the boat was for sale if he lived at the Island, she only put the card in Ripley's stores. Maggie closed the door and headed back into the kitchen. She picked up the envelope with the money and put it in a drawer where she also kept the bills that had been piling up. "Sorry Jack," she said under her breath and called Sam to come and take the drinks that she had prepared. Sam didn't answer. She walked through to the living room. The twins were still there playing with the bricks, but Sam was nowhere to be seen.

As she was leaving the room, she saw the leaflet on the coffee table. She picked it up to find Sam had written 'Changed my mind. Gone to Tod's, back later. Love Sam. X' Maggie looked through the netted curtains and saw that Sam's bike was not in its usual place, up against the shed.

Chapter 12

The Flying Fish was now far out on the Caribbean Sea, which was very calm, no wind. Ned was steering the boat with one hand and swigging from a small bottle of white rum from the other. Sam was in the cabin, hiding behind the curtain of the bed. There was a small tear in the curtain where Sam could keep a constant eye on Ned at the top of the small cabin stairs. This man Ned was hiding something, and Sam was going to find out.

Ned sang a song:

"Oh, she's a beauty She is the jewel of the sand

Oh, what a beauty

She is my treasure of the land."

As Sam sat on the cabin bed, he thought about the pile of money he saw on the table in the kitchen... the ransom money. Sam had it in his mind that this man Ned kidnapped Jack from the boat that night six weeks ago and had him tied up somewhere like the man he saw on TV.

He remembered Jack scribbling on the leaflet that morning, so he picked it up in the kitchen hoping it would give him some clues about the kidnapper, but the leaflet only had circles around the log advertisement and Jack had been writing how many logs he was going to buy and the cost. Ned drank the last drop from the bottle of rum and seeing that it was empty, he threw it overboard and turned the engine off. Sam observed Ned descend the stairs and grab another small bottle of rum from his white plastic bag that he left on the table. As Ned was about to go back upstairs, the bed where Sam was sitting, creaked.

"Who's there?" Ned said, as he turned. He retrieved a big knife from a drawer and approached the curtain. "Come on, show yourself." He reached out to the curtain and pulled it back.

Both Sam and Ned screamed simultaneously.

Sam looked frightened as Ned, the suspected kidnapper, was holding a big knife in the air ready to strike. Ned looked closer at Sam and slowly lowered his hand. "Aren't you Maggie's lad?"

"Yeh. I was playing on the boat earlier, I fell asleep." Ned looked at him suspiciously, he knew Sam was looking after the twins. "Why didn't you speak up earlier then lad?"

"I was scared, I didn't know what to do."

Ned scratched his head. "Well, I'll have to phone your mother. She'll be worried sick." He retrieved a card from his jacket pocket with the contact details on it and went to retrieve his mobile from the plastic bag, but discovered the battery was dead. "Damn!" he exclaimed. "What am I going to do now?" He ran back up the stairs to check the fuel gauge. It was very low, not enough to turn back and there was no wind to sail. He shouted back down the stairs. "Fuels too low lad. I'll have to refuel when we get to Turtle Bay. I'll phone your poor mother once I've recharged the phone at my house." 'Perfect,' Sam thought. When Ned's busy doing other things at the house, he would find his dad and cut him free.

Ned sat on the cabin's table, one leg up resting on

it, like the Italian man on TV. He was looking straight at Sam, who was still petrified of this man with the knife. Ned reached into his white plastic bag and pulled out a ripe peach. He started cutting it slowly and, with a piece on the knife, offered it to Sam. "Do you want some lad?" "No thanks," Sam moved further back on the bed. Ned put the peach slice in his mouth and started to bite into it. Peach juice began to dribble down his white beard. "When we get to my house and wait for the phone to charge, I'll cook up a gem of a fish dish. Would you like that lad, you must be hungry?"

Sam decided to play along. He didn't want to mess with the man with a knife. "Yeh," he replied.

"Ok," said Ned "I'll make that a promise then. I like mine slowly battered." He looked at Sam intently... "that's the fish. Then, when we wait for the authorities to pick you up, I'll show you how to hook a live maggot. I've got a bucket full of them in my garage." He looked more closely into Sam's grey eyes. "The ones that wriggle are the worst... slimy little suckers."

On the South side of Greenstone Island was a harbour. A ferry docked carrying cars, coaches and foot passengers. As the ferry disembarked a white van sped off and followed the road sign to Turtle Bay.

Later in the evening it started to rain. Sam was now lying flat on the cabin bed; he was feeling tired. Ned, back at the steering wheel, started singing his song about the jewel and treasure repeatedly as he took swigs from the rum bottle.

He called down into the cabin. "When we get to my house lad, don't be frightened of Minnie, she's a regular visitor from the lagoon. Funny little thing she is if you whistle, she comes running, just like a dog. If you are friendly to her, she will be friendly to you."

"I won't be frightened."

'Great,' thought Sam. Ned had an accomplice. This was going to be more difficult than he thought.

Sam was feeling very sleepy and started to get comfortable on the bed.

"Not long now lad, I'll ring Maggie from the house, and we'll have you back home in no time."

As Ned steered, he also thought about another call he was going to make. A call to the orphanage in Caracas. He wanted to find out if they had any old records of a child with fair hair and a certain feature on their face. When he saw the twin earlier that day, it was like looking at the child in Rosa's photograph that she had shown him all those years ago, the child Rosa said had died. There were three features common to the photo and the twin, blonde hair, green eyes and a small red birthmark on their chins.

His thoughts went back to Sam in the cabin and without looking round said.

"Now what was I talking about lad.... oh yes, Minnie. You know, my new housemate has really taken a shine to Minnie. If he's not taking long walks with her through the forest, he's carving wooden spoons and using them as drumsticks on my pots and pans. I've got a barrel full of those dam spoons, sometimes I wish I never bought him that penknife." Ned laughed, "He's a strange man, very strange indeed, doesn't say much but totally harmless. It was the same day I saw this boat. I was admiring it from the other side of the river as it passed me when I was fishing one evening. I often fish when it rains, you get a better catch. A few boats passed me by on the river that night, but when I saw this boat, it was by far the best. I was shopping in Ripley's last week, looking for some fishing tackle when I saw the card on the board, and it said the Flying Fish, I remembered the name of the boat, that was it, I knew I had to have it."

Six weeks previously, The Flying Fish went by as Ned admired it from the riverbank. It was raining and Ned was sitting fishing in a hunched position with a large dark waterproof sheet over his body. All Ned was looking at was the boat. He didn't see the dark hooded figure of Jack steering or Sam peering through the steamy porthole. "Anyway, about an hour after your boat went by, I saw something caught on a branch near where I was sitting, and I looked closer. It was a man clinging to a big red ball. My immediate thought was it must be another fisherman who had slipped from the bank, I almost slipped in myself, it was that muddy. I put my rod down, wadded over and pulled him out onto the bank. He was still conscious, lucky fella, but he had a big gash on his head. I searched for some ID but couldn't find anything. The only word he said to me was Woody, so I presumed it was his name. Anyway, I didn't have my phone with me and no one else was around to help so I put him in my small motorboat and took him to Greenstone. There's an excellent hospital there, much better than the one in San Pengio. After the hospital fixed him up, Woody came back to my house and he's been there ever since. He didn't have anywhere else to go. Must have some family somewhere that misses him eh, lad?"

Ned turned and looked down the stairs at Sam, but he was already fast asleep. The last thing Sam heard Ned say before falling fast asleep was about whistling for Minnie.

With a few miles to go before they reached Greenstone Island and with Sam fast asleep, Ned thought about the child in the photo and about Rosa, the woman that he hadn't seen for 15 years. He thought about the day after the office party of 1978, when security found him crashed out next to the firm's trash cans. He decided to quit the firm that day, he just didn't go back. He went back to the hotel and found Rosa had taken all her things, including her passport and left. He called her mobile but was getting no response.

After waiting for her to call, he decided to get the next plane back to Bogotá, thinking that she went home in a rage.

When he got back to the house, she wasn't there. He ran upstairs to the bedroom. Her clothes were still there, well most of them. Then the house phone started to ring. He quickly answered it from the line in the bedroom. It was the local clinic calling, wondering why Rosa hadn't been in for her yearly checkup that day.

"What?" enquired Ned, "for Botox injections?" "No," said the woman on the other end of the line.

"For her facelift and rib extraction."

At the end of the call, a shocked Ned walked over to Rosa's jewelry box and lifted the lid. All the expensive jewelry he had ever bought her was gone. He walked over to her wardrobe. The most expensive designer dresses, all gone. Ned had wondered at the time why her bags were so heavy as they left the house previously to fly to the office event in '78. Her excuse was, 'Not decide what wear'. Those scars she showed him once weren't for a hysterectomy as she described, but the result of having her damn ribs removed to make her waist thinner. Ned wondered how many other wealthy men she had robbed to pay for the surgery she had over the years.

As Ned steered the boat into Turtle Bay, he knew an even bigger lie was to be revealed. He was beginning to build a clear picture of Rosa Maria Gonzalez, and Ned was going to find out what she had been hiding all those years.

Chapter 13

When the Flying Fish pulled into Turtle Bay, Sam was still fast asleep on the cabin bed. It had stopped raining. Ned moored the Flying Fish behind an old wreck of a sailing boat and his small motorboat and turned the engine off. He put the keys into his jacket pocket and secured the boat. He was about to shout for Sam when he heard a vehicle screech to a halt outside his house which was overlooking the bay.

Curious, Ned walked up the jetty, as two men emerged from the white van. Ned was a bit unsteady on his feet due to the amount of rum he had consumed, and his vision was slightly blurred. He still had the bottle of rum in one hand. As Ned got nearer to the van, he saw that one of the men, the shorter of the two, was smoking. Even nearer, Ned realised who the smoking man was, he could never forget that grinning face.

It was him, John Bosman, CEO of South America Gems Inc. Boss, raising his straw trilby hat to reveal a bald head.

"Good evening Ned, long time no see."

Ned turned and started running to the other side of the bay, stumbling now and again. The two men walked slowly after him. Ned ran until he could run no further, a wall of high rocks blocked him in a corner. He stopped and turned to face the two men. Boss, now in his sixties, had put on a lot more weight since Ned saw him last.

Boss mopped his bald head with a handkerchief. He wore small round spectacles and was dressed in a baggy cream suit with a white shirt underneath. The tall man standing next to him was much younger, in his late 20s. He had a crew cut fair hair, clean shaven and was very well built. He was dressed in tight fitting stone coloured chinos and a white short sleeved T shirt exposing a tribal tattoo down one arm.

"Well now Ned," Boss said. "I was rather hoping you would be pleased to see me, but it seems from your reaction that the opposite is true. I am disappointed."

"What do you want?" asked Ned.

"Oh, just a little word. You know you were a hard man to track down at first. Then after a while, I thought back to the time when you were at the firm. When you spoke about a lovely Island that you knew of, and how you would like to retire there when the time came. Remember that Ned?"

"How did you know? I didn't tell you anything." "Oh, let's just say a little bird told me. I must say, from what I've seen so far, I can see what the attraction is. Might even get a place of my own. We could even be neighbours. What do you think about that?"

Ned grimaced.

Boss stubbed out his cigar with his shoe and walked towards Ned, putting an arm around his shoulder. "Look here Ned, we're good buddies aren't we. I came here to be friendly and talk to you about a little proposition of mine. Look I'll cut to the chase, I want you back at the firm. I'll pay you 5 times what I paid you before plus a few extra

bonuses thrown in, a bigger house, fancy cars, anything you want. Now come on, how can you refuse that buddy?"
"Nothing you say will interest me, you're wasting your time. I'm a fisherman now, and I'm happy."

"I miss you buddy, you were my finest geologist, we worked well together don't you think? You know, you should have stuck around. That mine in Bogotá turned out to be highly successful, it was the most profitable of all our mines."

"What do you mean was?"

"Oh, there's just one minor hitch, nothing we can't fix... together."

"Oh, is that what you call it, that's not what I heard." Boss walked away from Ned lighting another cigar. "And what have you heard about Ned?" taking a long drag.

"I saw the announcement on the mining channel. You're finished!"

Boss looked up to Ned's impressive house with its bay fronted windows. "What's going on here Ned? You seem to have done quite well for yourself on a fisherman's wage. What exactly are you fishing for... bluefin or perhaps it's something of a higher value? What is it about this Island that fascinates you so much that you even turn down a six-figure salary? It's funny, I seem to recall you talking about corrugated housing in your report, but all the houses I saw on the way here were quite satisfactory." Boss turned to face him.

"There's nothing for you here." "Oh, I think there is Ned."

Boss continued, "Do you remember that office party of 1978? No, you wouldn't, would you? You were so drunk security found you sleeping by the trash cans the following morning. Well, when you were busy cavorting with that tramp, oh what was her name now... Linzi I think, yes Linzi, I was having a nice long chat with your girlfriend Rosa. She was even chattier after a few glasses of champagne."

Ned remained silent. "She was telling me all sorts of things about you, that you took away her lucrative career."

"What lucrative career? She was my housekeeper."
"How she ran around for you like a perfect little slave, always at your beck and call. She said she couldn't stand being near you and your bad breath. She didn't know where you were or what you were doing at that party, not that she cared. Anyway, when you didn't show up later, I had to escort her back to your hotel room. Sweet quiet Rosa, who would have known, she was quite a vixen that night."

There was no reaction from Ned.

"The next day, I was back in the office feeling quite chirpy, as you do. I'd just been on the phone to HR telling them to show Linzi the door and arranging the trucks for the workers, and shortly after that, I received a call from Rosa. She was hysterical, saying she was sick of being treated like mud on your shoe, and that she had left you and wanted me to meet her at Dino's Diner. I went to meet her, took her to my residence, and haven't looked back since. We discovered we had a lot in common."

Ned spoke. "I'm sure you did."

"You see Ned, Rosa and I both enjoy the finer things in life. I was sick of chasing office bimbos and thought it was about time I settled down. With Rosa, one thing led to another and before we knew it…"

Boss wanted a reaction from Ned. "Goddammit man, I married her." Boss flashed the gold band on his finger at him. "She gets everything from me, expensive jewelry, designer clothes, luxury vacations, only the best for my sweet Rosa. When she knew I was looking for you, she mentioned this particular place on the bay, and said that you had spoken to her about it years ago. It had filled her with dread; she couldn't think of anything worse than being cut off from civilisation."

It's then that Ned started to laugh hysterically. "She got to me to get to you, don't you see? She did her research well. Heck, our pictures and autobiographies were plastered all over the national newspapers that time you received the award. Don't you see, she planned it all along. God knows how many other wealthy men she's robbed and fooled on the way to the top. She got what she wanted, the wealthiest man in South America. Just how long have you been together... must be nearly 15 years. She's fooled you for 15 years. Hats off to Rosa, what a lady. The woman you married is a manipulative, despicable liar and a thief, and she'll do anything to get what she wants. You know, she even told me that her child died, and she couldn't have any more children."

"What child?"

"Ah, of course she wouldn't tell you that. How many have you got, two? Three? My heart goes out to those poor souls having such a heartless mother like Rosa. Hahahaha."

Boss turned away, thinking as he rubbed the ring on his finger. He realised he was not going to get anything from Ned and turned to the young man who had been standing there the whole time listening. "Flex... take this drunken idiot out of my sight, then meet me at the house."

Boss looked towards the house and stubbed his cigar out on the ground. A light was on. "I'm gonna find out what he's been hiding on this island, and I have a fair idea what it is."

Flex grabbed Ned by the shoulder and dragged him into a dark corner of the rocks. As Boss headed towards the house, he took a photograph out of his wallet and looked at it. It was an old photo of Rosa and their three children. As he got closer to the house, he could hear music playing.

Chapter 14

The sun was rising over Turtle Bay and the white van was gone. Some early morning joggers, a young couple running along the bay came across a man badly beaten up lying by the rocks. He wasn't moving so the woman checked his pulse. Ned's clothes were soaked in alcohol and there was an empty bottle of rum beside him. The male jogger ran up to the beach house, the only residence around, to get help but no one answered the doorbell. He ran back to the rocks and they both carried the man to their jeep parked on the bay. They drove Ned to the Island's hospital just a few miles away.

Jack is tied up in a chair with his hands and feet bound. He has brown tape across his mouth. The room he is in is dark and damp. There are long hooks hanging from the ceiling. In the corner is a table where Ned is hitting a big fish with a giant mallet. Peach juice dribbles down his beard and fish guts are flying everywhere. Sam is walking through the room trying to reach Jack. As Sam gets closer to Jack, he sinks deeper into the sea of live maggots wriggling around his body.

Sam woke up in a sweat, panting heavily. Sunlight was pouring through the porthole. Once he pulled himself together after that bad nightmare, he rubbed his eyes and stretched. He saw Ned's phone still on the table, jumped off the bed and went up on deck. Looking around, the sea was calm, the bay deserted and there was no sign of Ned. He saw a house at the top of the bay. He shouted out for Ned several times, but there was no reply. Sam was puzzled why Ned hadn't tied him up as he had the opportunity when he was asleep. Then he thought Ned probably went to his house to fetch some rope. Sam must act quickly. He went back into the cabin and retrieved the big knife. He gave it a few practise swings, like the swords he saw on TV and proceeded to the house.

Sam reached the house and went to the front of it, where the bay windows were, but the blinds were closed. He put his ear to the window, he couldn't hear a thing. He went back to the side of the house and slowly pushed the heavy black door and it clicked open. Knife at the ready, Sam entered the house. The room was one large open space with a modern kitchen in one corner. Floor to ceiling windows covered one side of the room, where the blinds had been closed.

Sam said softly, "Dad, Dad?" There was no answer. The room was in a mess. Emptied drawers and their contents were scattered all over the floor, the leather furniture had been ripped apart with cushions scattered everywhere.

A bookshelf was lying on the floor, with fishing books strewn everywhere. A TV had been pushed off its stand, pots pans and cutlery all over the place. The only thing intact was a long aquatic tank on the other side of the wall to the windows.

Sam thought that Ned and his dad must have had a fight. Sam walked to another door and opened it and descended the steps. The steps led to Ned's garage. There was a blue van with 'Catch of The Day' written on the side of it and the back doors were open. Sam walked slowly towards the doors to see what was inside.

As he passed the passenger seats, he could see they had been torn out. He had to step over fishing gear which was strewn about on the floor along with pots of paints and pages of newspaper. As he reached the back of the van he flinched as he observed a swarm of live maggots near an overturned bucket. Knife still at the ready, Sam peered into the van. It was empty except for some wicker cages, buckets and fishing nets. Sam walked back into the main room where he first came into the house, over to the tank and peered inside. It was full of aquatic plants and rocks embedded in sand. As he peered closer a pair of dark eyes stared back at him through the glass causing Sam to jump backwards.

He looked closer inside the tank. Another pair of eyes appeared, then another and another. Then with the eyes came some pincers, opening and closing, scratching the side of the tank. From deep within the tank they all began to emerge. Sam counted eighteen large crabs and he watched them for a while slowly moving around the tank. Suddenly, Sam heard a loud thumping noise coming from a cupboard at the back of the kitchen.

"Dad!" Sam shouted. There was an even bigger thump against the cupboard door. Sam thought his dad was locked up in the cupboard with tape across his mouth, that's why he couldn't speak.

Sam cautiously approached the cupboard and slowly twisted the round handle which was covered in a sticky green slime. The handle clicked and almost immediately the door flew open. A large object jumped over Sam making him fall to the floor, the knife flew out of his hand to the other side of the room.

The object landed on the kitchen counter, at the same time a barrel containing wooden spoons spilt out of the cupboard. From where he was lying on the floor Sam was at the wrong angle to see what the object was. Petrified, he slowly raised his head. Whatever it was, was covered in a tea towel and flour. Sam took one corner of the towel, pulled it and ducked. Still there was no movement. Sam slowly raised his head and froze in fear when the object was on full display. It was the largest toad he had ever seen in his life, at least 2 feet high. Sam was afraid to even move from his spot.

A large glossy black beetle then scurried out of the same cupboard. The statuesque toad immediately shot out a long black tongue, scooped it up into its mouth and swallowed it down in one gulp. As Sam watched it, he remembered something that Ned said on the boat, just before he fell asleep.

"Don't be afraid of Minnie, she's a regular visitor from the lagoon."

In a soft voice Sam said, "Minnie?"

The toad let out a tremendous croak. Sam grabbed one of the wooden spoons that was near him, for defence and slowly got up. The toad still didn't move. Sam moved slowly backwards and sat on a stool holding the spoon, watching it, waiting for it to do something. Next to the toad on the counter was a portable CD player and a Phil Collins CD named In the Air Tonight and some overturned pans. As Sam sat there for what seemed like ages, he started looking at the spoon and he flipped it over.

There was a letter carved into it. Sam looked closer. His face looked puzzled when he saw a badly carved 'W' on the back of the spoon. Sam looked towards the other wooden spoons that spilled out on the floor and could see some of them with the same letter W carved into them.

He looked over to the barrel and saw part of a word where the barrel has rolled on its side, written in black paint. 'ODYS.' When he was sure that the toad was not a threat Sam walked over to the barrel and picked it up. He read the whole word 'WOODYS'. It was the name his dad said his band mates had called him when they chatted that afternoon on the boat. Sam was puzzled. Why would Ned, the kidnapper, have a barrel with his dad's name on it?

Near the barrel, on the wall was a pinboard and Sam spotted a photograph pinned to it. He pulled it off and looked at it closely. It was a photograph of Ned standing next to another man who had long unruly hair and a dark beard. Sam also saw a faint red gash on the forehead of the dark-haired bearded man. Both men had wide grins.

The dark-haired man was wearing a baggy cream shirt, just like Ned's shirt. They were standing in front of what looked like a lake holding a fish which must have been about 3 feet long. At the bottom of the picture Sam read the handwritten words 'The one that almost got away.'

He flipped the photo over. In scrawly handwriting it said, 'Ned and Woody fishing by the lagoon 15th August 1993'.

That was a week ago, thought Sam. He flipped the photo back and looked at the man with the dark beard again. He had deep blue eyes just like his dad. "Dad?" and then even louder, "Dad?" He realised it was his dad. Sam was not bothered by the toad now; he found his dad. As he jumped around the room waving the photograph in the air, he shouted, "Yes...yes...yes! I knew it. Dad's alive."

Minnie then let out the loudest croak ever. Sam wanted to phone his mum to let her know that Dad was alive, but there was no phone in the room. He didn't want to go back to the boat and wait for Ned's phone to charge, he didn't even know where the charger was. Looking at the photograph again, he decided to go and look for the lagoon, it couldn't be that far.

Jack might be fishing with Ned. Sam went to a tall fridge and took out two bottles labeled Greenstone Island Mineral Water and packed them along with the photograph and spoon into a small backpack he found in the room. He quickly checked out the two bedrooms of the house and he was even more convinced that Jack was alive when he found the checkered shirt his dad was wearing the day he disappeared.

As he left the house, Minnie leapt off the counter and hopped in front of him. She hopped down a sandy path lined with bushes. She knew the way to the lagoon. On the way to the lagoon Sam thought about the photograph again. His dad didn't look as though he was tied up at all, there wasn't a gun in Ned's hand and why were they both grinning. Sam's head was full of questions, but he was happy that his dad was alive and followed Minnie to the lagoon as fast as his legs would carry him.

Chapter 15

Twenty minutes later, they arrived at a blue lagoon surrounded by succulent green apple trees. The lagoon had a few large boulders scattered in it and Sam could see some small boats next to a hut in the distance. Across from the lagoon, on a hill was a dense green forest. Sam scrutinized the lagoon for any sign of his dad.

He shouted out, "Jack" a few times, but was met by silence. Disappointed and hungry, he picked a low hanging green apple, and sat on a rock by the lagoon biting into it. It was the juiciest apple he had ever tasted and much larger than the ones he was used to. It even tasted better than his favourite apples that his mum always bought from the market at San Pengio.

He watched as Minnie hopped from boulder to boulder on the lagoon until she was nearly on the other side where she stopped and stared at Sam as though expecting something from him.

"What do you want?" He shouted. "Croak."

Then he remembered something else that Ned had said on the boat. "If you whistle, she'll come running." Sam stood up, put two fingers in his mouth and whistled as loud as he could. Immediately, Minnie started hopping from boulder to boulder back to Sam. Sam took another bite of his apple as he watched her. She landed a small distance from his feet. "What?" he asked.

"Croak."

"I don't know what you want?"

Then, suddenly, Minnie shot out her long tongue and snatched the apple from Sam's hand, hopping with it back to the boulders. At the far end she stood on a boulder and dropped the apple into the water. Sam rolled about laughing. "Ned was right, you really are like a dog."

"Croak."

Sam picked more apples and played the game with her for a while, hoping his dad would show up. Then, exhausted, as Minnie was on a boulder catching and chasing the numerous dragonflies flying across the lagoon with her long tongue, Sam rested and opened a bottle of the Greenstone Island mineral water that he packed in the bag. As he took a long sip, the water on the lagoon appeared to sparkle on the surface.

The boulders turned into smaller rocks. The lagoon turned into a river, the same river which ran by Sam's house. Sam and Tod aged 8, were jumping from rock to rock across the river and throwing sticks of wood into it.

As Tod reached the bank, Sam followed behind him, lost his footing and fell into the river. The rapid current took Sam downstream towards the house. Tod ran along the riverbank shouting Sam's name. Sam couldn't swim and he was struggling to keep his head above the water.

Jack was out in the garden doing some woodwork when he heard Tod's screams. "Sam's in the river!" He shouted, pointing. Jack immediately dropped his tools and sprinted over to the river. He saw Sam coming downstream, his head disappearing from time to time, under the water. Jack dived into the river, swam to Sam and pulled him out onto the riverbank. Sam had stopped breathing. Jack gave him the kiss of life and pressed his chest as a hysterical Maggie ran to them from the house. After a few attempts from Jack, Sam spluttered out water, and started breathing again. Relieved, Jack and Maggie cradled him in their arms.

The river reverted to the blue lagoon. Sam looked at the bottle of water in his hand and exclaimed, "That's awesome."

He sat there for a while as he drank the water, planning what to do next and then he started thinking about home. He thought about his mum, and sisters Beth and Alice and how they would react when Sam told them that dad was alive. He imagined their happy faces. They could all go to Ripley's stores again, just like they used to, as one happy family. Ripley's was the biggest store in San Pengio, the store that sold anything and everything. On a family shopping trip, usually once a month, Sam would go with his Dad to the furniture department "Got to see what the competition is up to, son." he would always say.

In the furniture department Jack would even sneakily slip one of his business cards on their advertisement boards, he needed all the business he could get. While Sam and Jack were in the furniture department, Maggie would take the twins to the clothes department. She would always be on the lookout for bargains. Jack would say, "Go treat yourself hun," and would give her a handful of money, but she never did. She would always come back with a bag full of pretty dresses for the twins, trousers and tops for Sam, and more checkered shirts for Jack.

Whenever they left Ripley's and Jack went to fetch

the station wagon, as there was never any parking spaces left on the busy main road, Maggie would look through the window of JoJo's fashion stores next to Ripley's. Different dresses were displayed on the mannequins every month and each with a very high price tag. As Sam sat by the lagoon, he was looking forward to the day when the situation would return to normal and they could all go shopping together at Ripley's again. As he sat there, he also wondered if Ripley's had any Gameboys for sale.

Chapter 16

Sam looked back over the lagoon where Minnie was still chasing the dragon flies, when, out of nowhere, he heard the sound of a girl singing. He took the bag, got up and followed the sound. He didn't have to walk far, and he arrived at an area where there are even more fruit trees. Red apple trees, more green apple trees, orange trees, and mango trees. The area was abundant with vibrant wildflowers and green grass surrounding an old round stone wall.

Sam reached a bush where the red berries grew as big as grapes. He crouched behind it and observed the girl who was singing in the open grassy area. She had olive skin with long dark hair and wasn't much older than Sam. Her arms were outstretched as she sang and danced gracefully in a floating cream coloured dress like the ballerina Sam saw on TV once. He watched her for a while, singing and dancing, until he had to move a cramped leg. On doing so, the bush ruffled, and a few berries fell to the floor. On hearing the berries fall, the girl stopped singing and dancing, and looked over in the direction of the bush.

"Who's there?" she asked.

Sam knew he couldn't hide, sheepishly emerged from behind the bush and faced the girl. "Hi," he said nervously. The girl walked closer towards him, with her hands behind her back. "Were you watching me?" she asked.

"Er...yeh, I suppose," said Sam, he didn't know what to say. "Er, you're very good....at singing and dancing. You remind me of someone I saw on TV."

"Oh, really?" she said and held out her hand. "Well, I'm Mia, pleased to meet you."

Sam shook her hand. "Sam," he replied. Just then Minnie landed with a thud at Sam's feet as though she was protecting him. Mia frowned at the toad unphased.

"Oh, he's a fierce one and so protective."

"Her name is Minnie. Say hello to my new friend Mia."

Minnie croaked loudly and Sam and Mia laughed.

Shortly afterwards, Sam and Mia sat against the stoned round wall eating the red berries. Minnie had hopped back to the lagoon. "Why is everything here so juicy?" asked Sam, taking a bite of the berry.

"Because it's a magical place," replied Mia, "it's how I imagine heaven would be. I come here almost every day to sing and dance, it's my secret place."

"Magical?" questioned Sam inquisitively.

"Look I'll show you" Mia said as she stood up. "If you could have anything in the world, what would it be?"

Sam immediately answered, "To see my dad."

Mia looked a bit puzzled. "Ok, if that's what you want... stand up."

Sam obediently stood up.

"Look into the well," she said, pointing at the stone wall behind them.

"That's a well?" Sam questioned. Mia nods. "Ok then." Cynically, Sam peered over the wall of the well. A long way down, at the very bottom was a dark pool of water and some rocks. He turned and faced Mia. "Nothing there," he said.

"Try harder," Mia demanded. "Imagine your father in your mind."

"Ok then," Sam closed his eyes before looking in the well again and at the very bottom saw the face of a man with dark long hair, a beard and blue eyes, rippling in the water below. "Woaah!" Sam exclaimed, as he fell back off the wall.

"Told you it's a magical place didn't I," said Mia with a smug look on her face. "Now, tell me about your father." Sam took the photograph out of the bag and Mia looked at it. "I know them, that's Ned and Woody. I know their names as my grandfather told me." Sam looked at her, "You know them?"

"Yes, I see them by the lagoon sometimes, fishing, when I come here to dance. I don't think they see me, and I never speak to them."

"Is this man ok?" Sam said pointing at his dad. "He's not tied up or anything like that?"

"No," she replied puzzled. "Why would he be?"

"So, they look friendly together then?"

"I guess so," Mia continued. "I always see the older man, Ned, talking, the other one, your dad, he doesn't say much. They just sit there and fish. Occasionally I hear a loud shout as they catch a big one, and a splash as they throw it back into the lagoon, but that's about all. Oh, and they both come to the parties that we have every Saturday night to welcome the visitors to the Island. Ned cooks fish on the grille and your dad plays the drums in our band. He's very good."

"And today's Saturday," beams Sam.

"So, do you want to go to a party tonight?" Mia asked. Sam's eyes lit up. "You bet!"

"Then follow me."

As Sam followed her to the village he talked about his dad, about the stories that his dad told him on the boat. He told her how he thought his dad had been kidnapped by Ned and about the time Minnie jumped out of the cupboard.

Chapter 17

The white van had parked deep in the forest in an open area. There was a small wooden hut nearby. Flex was doing pull ups with ease on a long thick branch of a tree and next to him was half a bottle of water on the ground. Woody was crouched next to a tree stump banging it with two wooden spoons. He was wearing jeans over walking boots, and a baggy cream shirt. His long black hair hung around his bearded face. Boss was walking up and down kicking leaves and smoking a cigar. The gold wedding band was not on his finger. He turned and shouted at Woody. "I said emeralds, not evergreens you fool! I didn't expect to be driven around a forest for hours and hours on a wild goose chase."

Woody had directed them around the vast forest all night from one spot to the next until daybreak. Now that dawn had broken, the greenery of the leaves shone through the foliage of the forest. Woody looked up into the leaves of the evergreen trees which were abundant throughout the forest. "Beauty," he said, admiringly. Boss went and crouched down before him on one knee.

"Stop doing that!" He grabbed the spoons and threw them to the ground. "Are you crazy?"

Woody looked across to the spoons. Boss took him by his collar and shook him furiously. "What did that drunk tell you about the emeralds? Where are they?" Woody was nonresponsive and just stared at the spoons. Boss now irritated, threw him back and stood up. He took some binoculars that were hanging around his neck and scoured the valley below for clues. The binoculars stopped at a village. He shouted over to Flex who was still doing pull ups.

"Tie that idiot up in that hut over there, we'll deal with him later."

Flex immediately jumped down and marched over to Woody who had now stood up to retrieve the spoons. Flex pulled him with a firm grip on his shirt and dragged him to the hut, retrieving some rope from the van on the way. Woody shuffled along, constantly looking back at the spoons on the forest floor.

Boss looked through his binoculars again at the village, magnifying the view. He viewed many people walking up and down a busy street, with shops either side. "All done Boss." Flex said as he emerged from the hut, securing the door with the drop-down latch.

"We should have left that idiot with that slime ball you kicked into the pantry. This has been a complete waste of my time," said Boss. As he walked back towards the van, Boss spotted the spoons and kicked them hard into a pile of leaves. "Someone in that village must know something, and I'm gonna find out." They both got back in the van and it screeched away, down a hill in the direction of the village.

Chapter 18

Flex drove them along a street lined with shops that were busy with tourists and local islanders of Caribbean appearance. They passed buildings which were clearly named, a bank, a chemist, a supermarket, a restaurant and eventually the van stopped outside a three-storey house, with a sign hanging outside 'L'il Joey's B&B.'

There was also a glass covered pinboard next to the front door containing a card saying, 'Vacancies' along with some photographs. Boss ordered Flex to get their bags from the back of the van and approached the front door of the house which was open. He scrutinized the photographs of the villas on the pinboard and entered the house.

He approached a small reception area and banged the bell on the desk. In the background he could hear a TV, sounded like horse racing was on. He heard a man shout, "Come on Charlie Boy, you can do it."

There were some leaflets on the reception's desk. Boss looked at one as he waited, smoking a cigar. He was particularly interested in the map of the Island. As he waited, he looked around the drabby reception area and spotted a framed picture of a man on the wall and went over to it. There was a crucifix above the old photograph.

The man was of Caribbean appearance and had a small lamp banded to his head. He was wearing dark blue overalls which were very dusty and around his waist was a belt holding a pickaxe. Boss read the inscription at the bottom of the frame and returned to the reception area banging the bell several times.

"Service!!" A short man of Caribbean appearance in his 60s emerged from the back through a net of hanging beads, chewing gum. A stick in one hand supported his slightly bent body in the other hand he held a mobile phone. The man, L'il Joey looked agitated. A horse named Fools Gold had been leading for most of the race but now, coming up to the last hurdle, Fools Gold was neck to neck with Joey's horse Charlie Boy.

Joey had put a $80 bet on Charlie Boy to win earlier that day. Joey observed the smoking customer behind the counter and said in a strong Caribbean accent, "Can't you read that sign over there?"

Boss's eyes followed the direction of his pointed stick towards a 'No Smoking' sign on the wall. He then stubbed his cigar out in the tipping dish. Boss then raised his trilby hat and said, "Howdy."

Joey was beginning to dislike this man already. "How can I help you?" asked Joey, as he leant forward on his stick, chewing the gum.

Boss picked up a leaflet and opened it up displaying the page with the luxury villas and said, "What have you got that's available?"

Joey replied, "Those ones are only for sale and they are 50 miles away, we only do rooms here."

"Well, what rooms have you got then?"

"One minute, let me check." Joey opened a drawer under the counter full of keys and selected a key with a number 13 tag. He placed the key on the desk in front of Boss. "You're in luck, it's the only room we have left. We're very busy this time of year, what with it being festival season and all dat."

Just then, Flex walked in wheeling two small suitcases. Joey noticed his tattooed arm. "He's with me," said Boss.

Joey looked from Flex to Boss. "Business or pleasure?"

"What?"

"Are you here for business purposes or pleasure?"

"Pleasure," replied Boss.

"Well," said Joey, "that room only has single beds."

Boss threw him a look. "I'll take it," and took the keys. Joey passed him a visitors' book to complete. Boss grabbed a pen from a pot on the desk and began entering details.

Joey enquired, "Will you be staying here long?" Boss surveyed the shabby interior. "Hopefully not," as he continued to fill out the book. "One night should be enough."

"Then that will be fifty dollars... each... cash in advance. Room condiments are extra."

Boss finished entering details in the book and slammed the pen back into the pot. He withdrew a wallet from his jacket pocket and walked over to a window. He looked up and down the busy street as he removed two notes. He spotted a bar on the other side of the street called 'The L'il Bar & Grill'.

As he turned back to the desk, looking past the beaded curtain, through to the office at the back, he spotted a hi vis jacket, hard hat with a lamp attached and a respiratory mask hanging up and a pair of black dusty boots on the floor.

Joey followed his gaze. Boss threw the two fifty-dollar notes on the desk. "Quite a busy little operation you've got going here," Boss said.

"We have a good community spirit and like to keep our visitors happy," Joey replied. Boss picked up a leaflet and pointed to an area on the map that had been shaded in red. "What's this?"

Joey looked at it. "Oh, that's the swamp. You don't want to go there, it's dangerous."

Boss looked at Joey suspiciously. "Is that so old man?"

"The room's up those stairs, at the top turn right into a corridor and it's the last room on the right." As Boss followed Flex up a flight of stairs, Joey shouted, "I'll send the maid up with some fresh towels. Breakfast is at 8am." Once out of sight, Joey looked at the fake entry in the book and then up at the obscure security camera above the desk. He dialled a number saved on his mobile. When the person at the end picked up, he said, "Gather the men for a meeting at the usual place in half an hour, I've got something to show them. Oh and, who won the race?"

Joey smiled as he waved the phone in the air, "Good old Charlie Boy, he never lets me down." And returned to his office at the back. The next race was about to begin.

Chapter 19

Boss and Flex entered a room of two single beds. It was very basic with standard furniture and the bed linen was in various shades of brown. The drawn curtains were a matching shade. A portable TV with a built-in video player was on a table in front of the beds and there was a small fridge. On a desk was a kettle, some mugs, glasses, sachets, a packet of nuts and more leaflets. There was also a video tape labelled Greenstone Island Main Attractions. Flex picked up the packet of nuts, opened it, and threw one into his mouth. He opened another door to reveal a white suite consisting of a shower, sink and toilet. Back in the room, Boss lit a cigar, headed straight to the window and pulled the curtains back. A brick wall blocked any view of the outside.

He opened his suitcase, mainly packed with clean white shirts, and dug out a handgun. Flex looked at Boss in shock as he brandished the gun in the air. "Are you going to use that?"

"If I need to," replied Boss as he lay on the bed scrutinizing the gun in his hands. His mobile phone rang, and he could see it was Rosa calling. He didn't answer it. Flex proceeded to unpack his suitcase and neatly placed his carefully ironed clothes into drawers.

Boss said, "What are you doing? We're only staying for a night." He removed a small business card from his jacket pocket and read it. 'Fit people to fit the right job for you'. Just then there was a knock at the door. Boss sat up and threw the gun back into the suitcase hiding it under a pile of shirts. "Flex, get the door."

Flex stopped what he was doing, took the packet of nuts from the desk and went and opened the door. The pretty young Caribbean woman behind the door was dressed in a maid's uniform. She was holding some fresh white towels. She couldn't help but notice Flex's bulging biceps as he leaned against the frame of the door. Flex noticed a heart shaped diamond pendant around her neck. "Nice bling," he said, throwing another nut from the packet into his mouth.

In a sweet voice she said, "L'il Joey said you would be needing these," and the maid handed the towels to Flex. Flex took the towels and watched her walk seductively back down the corridor. She took a glimpse back, to see Flex staring at her, and smiled.

"Who was it?" Boss asked as Flex walked back in the room.

"The maid with the towels." He put them in the bathroom and continued unpacking, he couldn't get the pretty maid with the big brown eyes, off his mind.

Later, after a rest and while Flex was taking a shower, Boss turned on the TV and slotted in the video tape, pressing play on the remote control. He was hoping to find some clues as to the whereabouts of the emeralds. After observing the equipment in Joey's office and the photograph on the wall, he was even more convinced that the islanders were hiding something.

Once the video started to play, there was a welcoming

speech from L'il Joey. "Well, what a surprise, is there anything this guy doesn't do," Boss said under his breath.

The long speech was followed by a medley of the Island's attractions also narrated by Joey, including the blue lagoon, the evergreen forest, the turtles at Turtle Bay, the fishing harbour where the ferry came in, and the bustling market every Tuesday and Thursday where you could purchase the islands naturally grown fruit and vegetables. There was an extra-long part describing the luxury villas for sale in the North, each bespokely decorated with its own swimming pool and barbeque area. Boss was about to switch it off but stopped when a section came on about the L'il Bar and Grill, where a party was held every Saturday night to welcome visitors.

The handheld camera captured local people mingling with the holiday makers. Boss noticed a lot of the male locals were wearing gold Rolex watches. As the camera spanned further around the party goers, Boss spotted Ned in a chef's hat serving fish from a grill. At the back of him, Woody was playing drums in a band. He turned the TV off and lay flat on the bed, taking his spectacles off, thinking. Flex entered the room with a towel around his midriff, another towel drying his hair. There was a tattoo of an eagle that stretched across his muscly chest.

"Flex... get ready... we are going to a party and make yourself useful, pass me those nuts."

Flex's face lit up, he was more than ready for a party and he handed Boss the packet of nuts. Boss swallowed what was left in the packet down in one go. He held his throat as the nuts were very spicy and his face started to turn red. He rushed to the fridge and retrieved a small bottle of clear liquid, which he thought was water as he didn't put his spectacles back on. He drank it back in one gulp. Immediately after, he rushed into the bathroom to throw up. Curious, Flex picked up the clear bottle and read the label. It was a bottle of Greenstone white rum with 60% alcohol content.

Chapter 20

That afternoon, Sam and Mia were in the living room of the B&B which Mia's grandfather owned. Sam replaced the receiver of the house phone. "Any luck getting through to your mother?" asked Mia from the couch, where she was sipping lemonade.

"No, she's not at there, I'll try again later."

Sam started to look around the room. On one wall was a framed picture of Mia with two older people, both Caribbean, a man with a stick and a woman. Next to the frame was a glass fronted cabinet containing a variety of gold-plated trophies and shields. One trophy was in the shape of a couple embraced in a dancing position. At the bottom of the trophy Sam read 'Finalists of Greenstone Island Dance Competition 1990'.

Next to the trophies were several silver framed photographs of a couple dancing together in various poses. The tall man was dark skinned and dressed in an all in one black glittery costume with a red bolero jacket. The woman, of Latino appearance, had her black hair tied up into a neat bun and was dressed in a flowing red ballroom gown. "Who are these people?" asked Sam pointing at the silver framed photographs.

Mia slowly rose from her seated position and stood next to Sam, looking at the photographs one by one. "They are my parents" she said sadly, returning to the couch. Sam went and sat next to her. "My parents taught me how to dance from the day I could walk. We would often go up to that place where I met you near the lagoon to practise." She paused. "They were coming back from a dance competition three years ago. It was late at night and raining. Their car was hit by a truck as it took a bend in the hills."

"I'm sorry," said Sam, "you look a lot like your mother...who looks after you now?"

"L'il Joey, my grandfather. My grandmother used to live with us." She pointed to the framed photograph on the wall. "When my parents were alive, we all lived together, we were very happy, but after my parents died, Joey started gambling. Then after a couple of years and many arguments, my grandmother couldn't put up with it anymore and they recently separated. I go and visit her sometimes. She lives alone in a nice house in the North which Joey bought for her. Whenever I go there, she always asks me, is that man still gambling on those horses? He's going to gamble his life away. My grandfather doesn't say anything, but I know he misses her, and he's always buying her things for her house." Mia cheered up a bit. "Joey's always busy doing something or other, I hardly see him. I get lonely on my own so I go to that place by the lagoon as often as I can to relive those happy days... you see Sam, the reason I go there is to sing and dance with my dead parents."

Just then, Joey entered the room with a security video tape in one hand and shouted, "Mia where have you been? I've been looking for you. Have you been up at dat well again? How many times have I told..." Joey stopped in his tracks as he saw Sam sitting next to her. "Who dis?" he asked.

"It's my friend Sam, I met him by the well. He's the son of the man that plays drums."

"What man?" Asked Joey. Sam said, "Woody."

Joey looked shocked. "Ah, really? I didn't know Woody had a son." He hobbled over to Sam with his stick in his hand and bent down. He looked closely into Sam's eyes and tidy brown hair. "Does he say more than one word?"

"Of course I can!" Sam snapped.

Joey tutted and turned to Mia. "Have you finished doing those accounts I asked you to do?"

Mia got up and retrieved a rubber banded file from a desk which was covered in papers. "Here you are grandfather. I've listed all the receipts in date order, just as you asked."

"Good," said Joey as he took the file from her. "I've got to go to an important meeting, I'll be back later. Oh, and we have some new guests. I put dem in number thirteen. Stay away from dem, dey are bad news."

As he left the room with the file tucked under his arm, Joey thought about Woody. He pondered about Sam being Woody's son, the unspoken scruffy man that Ned had introduced once at the party as his own long-lost son.

Chapter 21

Later with his belly full of spicy chicken curry and rice, Sam, exhausted, fell asleep on the couch. Mia had cooked the meal for them earlier, showing him the step by step process. Tears flowed down Sam's face when his duty was to cut the onions.

When he woke up, the house was silent. As he sat up, he saw a handwritten note on the glass table in front of him. 'To Sleepyhead. Gone to help prepare for the party at the bar across the road. See you at 8pm sharp'. Sam looked at the clock on the wall. It was nearly eight o'clock. He remembered to phone his mum, and once through, it didn't ring for long as Maggie picked it up. "Mum, it's me Sam."

"Sam, where are you? You didn't go to Tod's" "I've found dad. He's alive"

"What Sam?"

"I've got to go Mum, I'm bringing Dad home. Love you, Mum."

"Sam, don't hang up..."

Sam put the phone down, quickly took the photo and the spoon from the backpack and ran out of the house to the L'il Bar and Grille across the road.

When Sam arrived at the open-air bar, a band was just setting up. There was no sign of his dad or Ned yet. Mia was cutting up fruit on a long table and helping two elderly women prepare some Caribbean punch. When Mia spotted Sam, she waved him over.

Boss and Flex arrived when the party was in full swing. The band was playing a medley of reggae songs. Holiday makers mingled with the locals, who were mainly women, dancing along to the music. Other local women dressed in colourful attire were serving drinks to the guests seated at tables, some with children.

A man at a grille cooked chicken and served it to a queue of people. Boss still had the same baggy cream suit on, he just changed his shirt, the same colour as the previous shirt, white. Flex wore sunglasses and a colourful short sleeved shirt hung loosely over a clean pair of faded blue jeans. Boss immediately started to scan the room for local men wearing Rolexes, but there were no local men to be seen other than the barman and the man at the grille. "Flex, go and mix, see what you can find out."

Flex was happy to mix as he had spotted a bevy of young island women at the dance area. Boss decided to head to the bar to get a drink and quiz the barman. At the bar, the barman approached Boss.

"Wa guan bedren?"

Boss responded, "Pardon?" "Whappen, Whe yu ah seh?"

Boss had no idea what the man was saying. "Tequila, and bring me the bottle"

The barman fetched a bottle of tequila, plonked it in front of Boss with a shot glass, and pointed to the pretty women on the dance floor, with a smile on his face.

"Jeezum peas"

"Sure." Boss opened his wallet and paid the barman.

He realised he wouldn't get very far due to the language barrier and took out the old photo of Rosa with their three children and put it on the bar. He dialled a saved number on his mobile phone and his attorney at the other end picked it up.

Looking at the photo, Boss said, "George. It's me. Now listen... and listen very carefully. There's something that I need you to do..."

After the long phone call, Boss sat at the bar for a while, drinking tequilas and smoking cigars, watching and waiting. Flex came up to him dripping in sweat. He ordered a strong cocktail and a bottle of water. "Well, have you found out anything yet?"

"No, nothing Boss."

"Well try harder then, I don't pay you for nothing." Flex took the drinks and headed back to join the party.

The maid who he met earlier, at the B&B, was amongst the group of women he had been dancing with and Flex was eager to get back to her. Then a group of elderly men walked in, some of them very frail. They glared at Boss with looks that would kill before joining their elderly female partners. L'il Joey arrived soon after. He was dwarfed by a group of younger, local men, the kind of men that you wouldn't want to mess with. The men had two things in common, they were all wearing gold Rolexes and black boots like the ones Boss saw earlier in Joey's office. The men slowly passed where Boss was seated, staring at him intently until they dispersed to find their partners. Two of the men headed towards the grille with Joey where Joey was the first to take a leg of cooked chicken. He then turned and faced Boss. The elders had something very interesting to say about the man in the security footage. Staring at Boss, Joey bit into the chicken leg and spat a piece of gristle to the floor.

It was evident to Boss that these men weren't going to give anything away. He took the leaflet out of his pocket and looked at the shaded area on the map situated on the west side of the island. He downed a couple more shots and went to find Flex with the leaflet in his hand.

With Boss defeated, Joey turned back to the man serving at the grille. "Where's Ned tonight?"

"He didn't show up." replied the man at the grille.

Joey dialled a saved number on his mobile phone and was greeted with an automated message "Gone fishing, back tomorrow."

As the band played Mr. Loverman, Boss spotted Flex dancing very closely with a young woman in a blue dress. Boss was not pleased. He was just about to go and drag him away when, at the corner of his eye he saw a young boy sitting on a bench watching the band. The thing that most caught Boss's eye was the wooden spoon sticking out of the boy's back pocket. Sam had been sitting there most of the evening, watching and waiting for his dad to show up. Mia had joined him occasionally to make sure he was ok, but she was also busy serving drinks and food to the party goers.

"Howdy," Boss lifted his hat as he took a seat next to Sam.

"Hi," Sam replied.

"Enjoying the party boy?" Boss said, lighting a cigar. "No."

"Why's that then boy?" "My dad hasn't shown up."

"Is that so?" Boss looked at the spoon in Sam's back pocket again. "What's that in your pocket?" knowing full well what it was. As Sam took the spoon out of his pocket, the photograph also fell out to the ground. Sam held both the spoon and photo in his hands. As Sam twisted the handle of the spoon round and round, Boss saw the letter W carved into it. Boss then looked at the photo of Ned and Woody. "You know Ned then boy?"

"Yeh, he kidnapped my dad." "Really?"

"Yeh, all he does is get drunk and sing about stupid treasure and a jewel all the time."

Boss's ears perked up. "A jewel you say boy. What kind of jewel?"

"I don't know... any jewel."

"Did he say anything else about the jewel?" "No, why?"

Boss thought this boy knew something and he was going to get it out of him one way or another. "Can I see that photo?" Sam showed the photograph to Boss. Boss pointed to Woody. "Is that your dad?"

"Yeh."

Boss looked at the log advertisement on the leaflet in his other hand and had a thought. "You know boy, Ned is a friend of mine." Sam looked at Boss curiously. "Yeh, we used to work together, we were great buddies. I'm sure he wouldn't do such a bad thing as kidnapping. Let me see that photo again. Well my boy, I think today might be your lucky day. You see, me and my friend over there," he pointed to Flex dancing, "we were walking in the forest today, admiring its beautiful greenery when we saw a man sitting outside a hut. He had a small bonfire going, had a.... a... rabbit on a skewer. Anyway, I went up to him and asked him for a light for my cigar, you see I'd forgotten to bring my lighter on the walk, and I was desperate." He looked more closely at the photo. "I could swear it was this man. In fact, I'm absolutely certain it was him."

"Yeh," Sam said excitedly. "Was it really him?" "Yeh I'm absolutely certain. In fact..." he stood up and called Flex over. The maid was taking polaroid pictures of them dancing together. Flex obediently ran over. "Look at this man Flex," as he pointed to Woody. "Would you say that's the man we saw sitting in the forest today?" Flex huffed and puffed and bent down for a closer look.

"Yeh, that's the guy I..." Boss jabbed him in the ribs with his elbow.

"That will be all, you can go now."

Alone again with Sam, Boss said, "I could take you to him. He's probably living in that hut. I think I remember where we saw him, just up a dirt track, can't be that hard to find. Would you like that boy?"

Sam looked over at the band who were now packing up, as it was nearly two in the morning. "Yes, take me there. I want to see my dad."

"Ok, I'll take you, but there's something else about this man I think you should know."

"What's that?" asked Sam.

"By the side of the hut was a pile of logs, stacked almost as high as a tree. He tried to sell me some when I asked him for a light. Hey, we've all got to try and make a living, but what he's doing is illegal, cutting down those beautiful trees and selling the wood like that. We'll have to keep this our little secret. You wouldn't want to see your dad getting into trouble with the law now, would we boy?"

"No."

Sam remembered that Jack wanted to see logs on the island, so he found Boss's story quite believable. Boss got up and approached Flex who was now sitting on a chair smoking a joint, with the maid on his lap caressing his head. As soon as he saw Boss approach he got up, chucked the joint and threw the maid flying to the floor. "Quick," said Boss, "we're leaving. Go and get our luggage from the room. Me and my little friend here will meet you by the van." Flex immediately left.

As Boss was leaving the bar with Sam, Mia ran up to them. "Where are you going Sam?"

"Oh, he's with me. Right little rascal this one, always getting into trouble," Boss said, ruffling Sam's hair. "Tells all sorts of stories about kidnapping and jewels." Boss fake laughed. "My brother found this leaflet in his bedroom, we put two and two together, and my brother told me to bring him back to the mainland. Gonna get the ferry and take him back where he belongs."

Mia turned to Sam. "Is that true?" "Yeh, sorry Mia. Bye."

"Bye Sam." As they walked away, Mia watched them thinking, the well never lied.

Later, when most of the people had gone, Joey, who had been talking with the partygoers for much of the night, approached Mia picking his teeth with a toothpick. Mia was helping to clear up. "Where's your little friend?" asked Joey. "Oh, you mean, Sam... he left earlier with a man... said he was his uncle, coming to pick him up and take him home on the ferry." Joey looked at his watch. The ferry didn't leave until 7am. He asked Mia what the man looked like. As Mia described the man, Joey's toothpick dropped out of his mouth. She's never seen Joey move so fast as he scurried out of the bar to the road, where he saw their white van parked earlier. The van had gone. He scurried into the house, up the stairs and along the corridor to number thirteen. The door was wide open. The men had already left, taking all their belongings with them.

Mia shortly appeared in the corridor. "Mia" Joey shouted "Quick, call the police!"

Chapter 22

The van arrived at the hut area in the forest. Boss, Sam and Flex were sitting at the front of the van. Sam couldn't wait to get out. "Calm down boy," said Boss, "all in good time."

They descended from the van and Sam ran to the hut banging on the wooden door trying to open it, but it didn't budge as there was a latch on the door. Sam tried to lift it, but it was too heavy. He didn't understand why a latch would be on it. "Dad! Dad! It's me, Sam!" and continued to bang on the door. Boss and Flex walked slowly towards the hut as Boss explained his plan to Flex. When they reached the door, Boss indicated to Flex to lift the latch. As the door opened, Sam ran inside the hut. There was nothing inside but a piece of rope which has been cut and a screwed up piece of masking tape. There was no sign of a knife. A window at the back of the hut was shattered. Sam didn't understand what was going on. "Where is he... where's my dad?"

Boss looked around the empty room then at Flex. "Yes Flex, where is he?"

"I don't know Boss, I tied...."

"Shut up!" shouted Boss, who then turned to Sam. "Seems I was wrong about Ned, my boy. He is a kidnapper, just like you said."

"Where's he taken him? Where's he taken my dad?"

Boss walked over to Flex and whispered, "Go look outside you idiot, he couldn't have got far." Boss then placed his hand around Sam's shoulder, "Don't worry boy, we'll find him," and led him outside kicking the rope on his way.

As Boss walked back outside, he spotted a dark figure in the distance silhouetted against the moonlit sky. Someone was sitting under a tree. "Flex," he whispered, "over there." Flex looked in the direction Boss was pointing and crept up to the spot where he found Woody fast asleep against a tree clutching the two wooden spoons to his chest, the wooden spoons that Boss had earlier kicked into the leaves. Woody's hands were covered in dirt, where he had been searching for them.

Boss walked up, still with his arm around Sam. "Well I'll be damned."

"Dad, Dad!" shouted Sam. He broke free from Boss and threw himself on Woody, hugging him, sobbing uncontrollably. Woody woke up and looked at this person on him. He pushed him away, guarding the spoons in his hands. "Dad, It's me Sam, your son." Woody looked at him blankly, then looked up to Boss and Flex who were just standing there, watching. Woody flinched and pulled the spoons closer to his chest. He spotted the spoon in Sam's back pocket and pointed to it. Sam followed his stare and took it out. Woody immediately snatched it from him and held it with the other two in his hand. "I found that spoon at Ned's house." Sam also showed him the photograph he found.

"Fish," is all Woody could say.

Boss looked towards Flex. "See, I told you that boy knows something, he's been to Ned's house."

"Dad, Mum misses you, and Beth and Alice, we all miss you, I can take you home now." Still all Sam was getting was a blank stare from Woody. Sam turned to Boss. "What has Ned done to him? Why won't he talk to me?"

"I don't know boy. But from the look of that nasty red mark on his head, I'm thinking it's something very bad. Look, let's all get back in the van. We'll take you to the authorities and they can deal with it all. They will get you home, find Ned and get him locked up."

Back in the van with Sam and Woody in the back, Boss looked at the shaded area of the map and showed Flex who was in the driver's seat. Flex gave an affirmative nod, switched on the ignition and the van sped off down the hill.

In the back of the van, Sam cuddled up next to Woody who sat in silence. He was still guarding the spoons. After a long bumpy drive, Sam heard the back doors unlock.

Chapter 23

Dawn was breaking as Sam and Woody got out of the van. Sam saw Boss standing by a barbed wire fence. There were signs strung along the fence saying 'Danger Swamp'... 'Do Not Enter'... 'Keep Out'. Boss retrieved a heavy rock from the base of the fence and chucked it over. As soon as the rock hit the muddy sludge it sank. Under his breath he said, "That old man was actually telling the truth." referring to his conversation with L'il Joey at the B&B.

"What's this?" asked Sam, looking around the area. "This isn't the police station. What's going on?"

"Flex... go get the wire cutters from the van." As Boss walked towards Sam, Flex went to fetch the wire cutters and some thick gloves. "Now look here boy," he said. "I was hoping to find something here, but unfortunately, it's just a swamp and that's not good news for you."

"What do you mean? Where are the police?"

"Look boy," Boss grabbed Sam's shoulder. "You have something that I want. If I don't get it..." he looked at Woody, who was just standing there with the spoons, then towards the swamp. "Well, a very bad thing is gonna happen. Do you understand?"

"I don't know what you're talking about."

"Do I have to spell it out for you? The emeralds, where are they. What did that drunk Ned tell you?"

"He didn't tell me about any emeralds." Then something twigged with Sam. "You're the one, aren't you? You're the one that kidnapped my dad and tied him up in that hut. He wasn't selling logs, you made it all up. You're the one that wrecked Ned's place. Aren't you... aren't you?"

"Didn't your parents ever teach you never to speak to strangers' boy?"

Sam started hitting Boss hard with his fists. "You did this to my dad. I'm going to kill you."

"Flex!" Boss shouted, taking hold of Sam's wrists. "Bring the rope!"

With Sam tied up around his wrists and Boss holding him back, Flex cut a man-sized hole in the fence and walked back to the group throwing the cutters and gloves on the ground. "Hold the boy," Boss said, snatching a spoon out of Woody's hand. Boss mimicked throwing it into the swamp. Sam looked at Woody as his eyes followed the spoon.

"No... no..." Sam shouted at Boss as he struggled in Flex's grip.

"Are you going to cooperate with me and tell me where the emeralds are boy... or not?" Boss waved the spoon again.

"I don't know what you're talking about. Ned didn't tell me anything. Please don't," Sam cried.

"Oh, what's the use?" Boss chucked the spoon with full force, over the fence and into the swamp. Woody immediately shuffled along towards the swamp to retrieve the spoon. "No, Dad no! Stop him." He was trying to break free from Flex's grip, who held Sam tightly around the waist. Then, from nowhere, a thought suddenly came into Sam's mind, "Okay, okay. I'll show you where your precious emeralds are."

"Excellent boy. I knew you wouldn't let me down." Boss indicated to Flex to go after Woody who was now halfway through the hole in the fence. Relieved, Flex immediately dropped Sam to the ground, ran to Woody, and pulled him back by his shirt. Another step and Woody would have been in the swamp. Once Sam could see that Woody was safe, he looked up at the grinning face of Boss. In Sam's mind, he was starting to formulate a plan.

Chapter 24

Another long drive, they arrived at the well. Sam hoped that Mia would turn up, see them and get the police. Woody was tied tightly to the trunk of a tree; he still held the remaining two spoons in his hands. He had been acting even crazier since that spoon went in the swamp. Boss looked around the deserted area. He checked the gun was in his holster as Joey's henchmen could show up at any minute. He turned to Sam who still had his hands tied, "So where are they then boy?"

"Over there, in the well," as he nodded in the direction of the well.

"Go take a look Flex," demanded Boss.

Flex went over to the well, jumped up onto the stone wall and peered down into the murky water at the bottom. For a moment he thought he saw the faint vision of the maid seductively looking up to him. She appeared to be dressed in a red bikini. Flex looked at the bottle of water in his hand, blinked a few times, looked again and the vision had gone. "Well, did you see anything?"

"Er....nothing Boss" As he jumped back off the wall he looked back again, puzzled.

Boss turned to Sam. "What is this boy, another wild goose chase? I want to see my emeralds, do you understand?"

"He didn't look close enough, why don't you go see for yourself?"

"Alright, but if you're playing silly games with me, we go back to that swamp."

Boss marched to the well, pushed Flex out of the way and looked over the wall. He looked back at Sam with an amazed look on his face and then looked down into the well again. At the bottom of the well he saw one large glowing emerald surrounded by lots of smaller ones. Sam stood and watched his reaction with a smug look on his face.

"How can you not see that down there idiot?" Boss said to Flex as he inspected a rusty metal ladder attached to one side of the well.

Flex was eager to look into the well again. On looking, he saw the vision of the maid again. "Oh, I see it Boss!"

Boss beckoned Sam over to the well.

Sam climbed down the metal ladder with a torch in his untied hands. He was the only one small enough to fit in the well and was ordered to retrieve the large emerald from the bottom. The well was dark and damp and had water marks on it where the well had become shallower over the years. When Sam reached the bottom, it was very dark. He saw the light at the top of the well where Boss and Flex looked down.

Sam used the torch to retrieve the large mossy rock from the cold murky water, the rock was surrounded by pebbles. Sam sat there for a while wondering how he was going to pull this one off. Boss shouted from the top of the well. "Hurry up boy, I haven't got all day."

As Sam sat there holding the mossy rock, he thought about how his dad could have ended up in the swamp. Tears started to roll down his cheeks. He wanted his dad back with the family, with everything being back to how it was before. That's when he heard a sound. A sound that echoed around the well. It was the sound of his dad saying, "I will always be there for you, Maggie and the twins, we're family." It was what his dad told him that day on the boat when they went sailing.

As Sam looked around the well, to find where the sound had come from, he heard another sound....a fluttering sound. Sam looked up and that's when he saw it. There was a colourful blue butterfly hovering above his head. Sam watched it for a while until it landed on the mossy rock in his hand. The rock immediately started to glow a brighter green, simultaneously Sam felt a force shoot through his body. His hand rose as the glowing rock pulled him up slowly through the well, transitioning into a brighter green as it rose higher.

Once Sam was over the well's wall and safely to the ground, the butterfly flew away. Sam dropped the torch and stood paralysed with the transitioned emerald in his outstretched hand, he had no control over what was happening to him. Flex and Boss were standing by the van talking, with their backs to Sam, they turned on hearing Sam return from the well.

"Well done boy," Boss said as he observed the green emerald in Sam's hand. As the men started walking towards him, Sam's head turned demonically towards a nearby apple tree. Two large apples dislodged from the branch and floated in the air towards Sam. The emerald rose from Sam's hand, and with the apples the three objects moved in front of Sam in a juggling pattern. As Flex looked in amazement, Boss stopped in his tracks. "What trickery is this?"

Sam's hands rose to his face, two fingers into his mouth. He whistled loudly. A few seconds later, Minnie landed with a thump in front of him, looking fiercer than ever. She squirted a huge sludge of green slime at the two men, rolled out her long black tongue, and grabbed the emerald from the air. The apples dropped to the ground as she hopped with the emerald wrapped in her tongue towards the lagoon. Boss wiped the green slime from his face with a tissue and removed the gun from its holster. "Watch the boy!" he shouted at Flex as he chased the toad brandishing the gun.

He gave Sam an angry look as he ran past him. As the force left Sam's body, he went limp. Flex, covered head to toe in slime, took what he thought was a possessed boy and quickly tied him next to Woody at the foot of the tree. "Goddam slimeball."

Flex uttered under his breath as he wiped the green slime from his clothes. He then ran back to the van to change. As Sam sat next to Woody with his long dark hair covering his face, he thought about all that had just happened, that he had no control over. He still hadn't got his dad back, not in the way Sam had hoped. Then he saw the butterfly again, hovering around the top of the well. Then it was joined by another one, then another until a hoard of blue butterflies came flying out of the well, into the blue sky. As Sam looked at them in wonderment, he heard a deep voice next to him. "Sam?"

Sam turned slowly to see Jack's blue eyes staring right at him, through a mass of dark hair. "Dad?" Sam's face lit up.

"Where are we? What's going on? Where's the boat?" Jack said, trying to break free from the rope.

Sam threw his bound body as near as he could to Jack, with tears of joy shouting. "You've come back, you've come back. I can't believe it."

After the situation had calmed down and Sam had told Jack about Boss, the well, the butterfly, the rock that turned into an emerald, the voice, the juggling apples and the giant toad, Jack responded "O... K. I believe you son." Jack looked up as Flex returned from the van with clean clothes on, combing his wet hair. He looked over to Jack and Sam to check they were still tied to the tree, then jumped up on the wall of the well and sat crossed legged on the rim. He was holding a photograph. As he was looking inside the well, Jack said to Sam, "Who's that numbskull?"

"That's Flex. He's the one that tied you up in a hut." As Sam looked at Jack something caught his eye, the object flickered in the midday sun. Sam looked down. The object that flickered was the blade of a penknife and it was at the back of Jack's boot, the same place he used to keep it as a boy.

A few minutes later, Flex was still at the well. He found a large rock and was exercising his biceps. The rope hung loosely around Sam and Jack's waists and wrists. "Hey you, big boy over there!" shouted Jack.

Flex looked around, put the photograph in his shirt pocket, threw the rock to the ground and jumped from the well. He marched across to where they were sitting. "You say something boy?" he said, looking at Sam. He didn't notice that the two wooden spoons Jack had been holding all along were now in Sam's 'tied' hands and that Jack's sleeves were rolled up.

Flex then looked at Jack and said, "What are you looking at?" Flex watched the loose rope as it dropped to the base of their feet as Sam and Jack stood up.

"My fist..." Jack pulled back one arm and as it landed flat on Flex, "in your face." Flex fell straight backwards to the ground; he was out in one punch.

"Way to go Dad!" shouted Sam proudly waving his arms in the air. As Jack checked Flex was out for the count, they heard the sound of a gun going off. "Come on dad. We have to save Minnie."

As Jack followed Sam running to the lagoon, Jack shouted, "Who's Minnie?" In their rush to save Minnie, they had forgotten to take the penknife which still lay at the base of the tree.

Chapter 25

Sam and Jack arrived at the lagoon. In the distance they saw Boss in a rowing boat. Now and again he was firing the gun at Minnie who was hopping from boulder to boulder. Sam pointed to the toad on a boulder "There's Minnie!"

"Minnie's a toad?" said Jack confused. Jack spotted a bunch of life jackets by the side of the lagoon near a hut and shouted to Sam, "You'd better take a life jacket son." "I don't need one. Come on Dad, we've got to hurry." Sam was already pushing another rowing boat onto the water. Jack climbed into the boat with Sam and took the oars. Boss fired his last shot at Minnie which missed and in anger, he chucked the gun into the lagoon. Once Jack saw that the gun went in the water, he upped the pace of his rowing whilst Sam told Jack about another little plan he had. Boss had grabbed his own oars and was rowing towards Minnie who was now standing statuesque on a boulder, the glowing emerald was still wrapped in her tongue.

When Jack and Sam reached Boss's boat, he stopped rowing. Sam was waving a wooden spoon in the air and Jack was trying to grab it. "Where's Flex?" asked Boss.

"We escaped," Sam said. "He didn't tie us up properly."

"Damn idiot," Boss made a mental note to have Flex

dismissed when he got back to the mainland. As he looked over at the toad with the emerald on the rock, Boss had a plan of his own. Boss walked nearer to the other boat and when Sam wasn't looking, leaned forward and snatched the spoon from his hand. Boss was surprised how easy it was, he didn't see Jack and Sam smiling at each other. Boss hid the spoon in an inside pocket, he will use it later to get Woody back... with his emerald.

He then picked up a long piece of wood that he saw earlier in the boat. Jack climbed onto Bosses boat with his head hung low. Boss turned as he hid the piece of wood behind his back. "Give me my spoon," Jack said in a muffled voice as he raised his head. Boss was shocked.

"It speaks more than one word. I am impressed." He continued, "Sure, you can have your spoon back." and he threw the piece of wood towards the boulder where Minnie sat. It landed with a splash near the rock. Boss turned to Jack. "Go get it then, what are you waiting for?"

Jack didn't respond. Just then a large splash occurred as Minnie dropped the emerald into the clear water of the lagoon. Sam, Jack and Boss looked around in amazement as the whole lagoon slowly transitioned from blue to a bright green, and below the water appeared thousands of sparkling emeralds. Boss was ecstatic, and he knelt looking over the edge of the boat to get a closer look.

Sam whispered over to Jack, "Dad, they're not real."
"Really?" Jack questioned.
"Really," Sam replied, "believe me, I'll explain later."
"Ok son," Jack said, grabbing an oar.

Seeing Jack with the oar, Boss stood up. "Oh, so you want your little wooden spoon, do you? You can have it." He retrieved it from his pocket and threw it at Jack's feet. "I've got what I want," he said, looking out at the emeralds again. Jack stepped over the spoon and went nearer to Boss. Boss said, "What now? I've given you your spoon back haven't I?"

Jack said in his normal voice, "I'll tell you what I want." Boss looked at Jack, mouth aghast. "My life back!" As Jack swung the oar, it hit Boss on the side of his belly and the boat wobbled. As Boss was knocked into the water, Jack lost his balance and hit his head on the side of the boat as he too fell in.

Sam rushed to the side of the other boat, and leaned over crying out, "Dad, Dad!" as the water reverted from green to blue. In the water, Boss was searching around the bed of the lagoon. All he could see and feel were mossy green rocks. Then from out of nowhere a fish nearly 3 feet long struck him, then another and another. They knocked Boss's glasses off.

Blind and exhausted, Boss returned to the surface of the water. Sam saw Boss emerge but there's no sign of Jack. Sam stood up and dived into the water. He swam to the bottom looking for Jack and spotted him a short distance away. When Sam reached Jack, he saw Jack pulling at his leg which was entangled in reeds. The more Jack pulled, the tighter the reeds got around his leg. Sam swam to his leg and tried to untangle Jack's foot, but it wouldn't budge. He remembered the penknife and searched in Jack's boot. It wasn't there. Sam looked up at Jack, he was losing air fast. Desperately, Sam searched around the bed of the lagoon. He found a long stone with a sharp edge and grabbed it. He used the sharp edge to try and cut away at the reeds. When he looked at Jack again, his eyes were starting to close. Sam cut faster and faster.

Eventually the reeds broke away and Sam dragged Jack back to the surface, leaning him against the side of the boat. Jack coughed as he caught his breath back. Sam looked at Jack concerned as there was another bleeding gash on his head where he hit the rowing boat. Panting, Jack turned to Sam and said, "Thanks son."

Sam smiled, breathing a sigh of relief. "Dad look!" Sam pointed to Minnie who was still on the boulder. She has been joined by another giant toad. They both laughed.

Chapter 26

Back safely on the boat with Jack recovering, they saw a speedboat with two police officers and a frogman dragging Boss out of the water. Sam and Jack looked over to the shore where a group of people had gathered. Sam took control of the oars and rowed the boat towards them.

Nearer the shore, Sam spotted Mia and L'il Joey standing with a group of men, the same men who were at the party. Then another figure appeared through the crowd, a woman. "Look Dad," Sam shouted at the top of his voice.

Jack looked over and was overwhelmed with joy as he saw Maggie. As they descended from the boat, a smiling Maggie came forward with an arm outstretched. "Jack," she said softly, "you forgot something." She opened her hand to reveal Jack's wallet. They ran to each other, kissed and embraced. Sam ran over and they all had one big hug. Afterwards, Maggie told Jack that the twins were in safe hands with Martha and Dan on the mainland and they rejoined the group of happy people watching them.

The crowd watched as Boss disembarked the speedboat with two policemen at his side. He shook the water from his hat and placed it back on his head before a policeman handcuffed him. The frogman was carrying the gun he found in the lagoon. As Boss passed the men in the crowd wearing Rolexes, Joey came forward and leaned on his stick. "You owe me... for the room condiments." Boss replied, "Speak to my assistant."

Joey learned from the police that Boss was a wanted man and they had been searching for him on the mainland. As CEO, he was responsible for a mine that collapsed in Bogotá three months previously as it didn't have the correct safety standards.

Joey's brother worked at the mine in 1982 as did many of the elders of the village, who had recognised Boss's face in the security footage. Due to the terrible working conditions, Joey's brother caught pneumonia and died. The framed photo below the crucifix in Joey's reception was his brother. Boss knew he worked in the Bogotá mine as that was what was inscribed at the bottom of the frame.

Another policeman came forward from the crowd. We found these, as he handed Jack the two spoons and the penknife. Jack looked at the back of the penknife. It had 'Woodys' inscribed into it. The crowd continued to watch as Boss was escorted to a second police car. In the other car a grim looking Flex was sitting at the back. He had a plaster over his nose and was holding a polaroid photo of the maid in his cuffed hands.

Sam went over to Mia and excitedly told her of the adventure he had from start to finish, the truth this time. He was also excited about telling the story to Tod when he got home. Maggie looked at Jack, at the bleeding gash on his head. "We'd better get you to the local hospital and get that checked out, and when we get home..." she touched his long hair and beard, "I'm getting the scissors out!" Jack agreed as he took her hand.

Chapter 27

Greenstone General was a clean, modern hospital. Sam sat and waited, outside a room where Maggie held Jack's hand as a nurse carefully bandaged his head. Sam watched as busy doctors of Caribbean appearance walked backwards and forwards along a corridor. They all wore clean white coats with stethoscopes around their necks and were carrying clipboards. A young unconscious woman was wheeled in and stopped in front of Sam when a doctor approached her. She was wearing a blue dress and a diamond heart pendant hung around her neck.

The uniformed man pushing her said, "She was found unresponsive this morning, suspected alcohol poisoning." The doctor checked her pulse and used a small light to look into her eyes.

"Give her some fluids and take her to ICU immediately." And she was wheeled away. Bored waiting, Sam jumped from the chair and started wandering along the corridor, reading the small boards posted outside each of the patients' rooms. He stopped at a particular room and peered through the small window. As a bandaged Jack and Maggie walked towards him, Sam pointed to the board. Written on the board was the name Edward Jenkins.

"Dad, it's the man that bought your boat, it's Ned."

Jack and Maggie came up to Sam and peered through the window. Ned was sitting up in bed with a tube leading to his arm, reading The Angling News. His face was covered in bruises. Maggie opened the door, and they all walked in. Ned lowered the newspaper. He didn't believe what he was seeing. "Maggie? Sam?" and then he paused for a moment. "Woody?"

"Hello Ned," said Maggie. "This is my husband Jack."

Ned looked puzzled. "Jack?"

Sam, Maggie and Ned chatted, exchanging their stories with Sam doing most of the talking. As they talked, Jack observed Ned. He looked at Ned's brass buttoned blue jacket slung over one chair and the cap and red cravat on the table. He didn't remember Ned from his days at the beach house. He didn't remember anything from the day he was hit by the boat's mask, that night until the day he first spoke to Sam under the tree. But he knew this man sitting there in the bed, with the white hair and the white beard.

It was the morning weeks ago, before the tragedy, when Jack was in San Pengio and he saw the line of people at a stall queuing for the cheap crab meat. He knew it was crab meat as there was a handwritten sign hanging from the stall. The capped white-haired man wearing a red cravat and blue jacket was behind the stall. Some fishing rods were propped up in one corner. He was busy taking ripped pages of newspaper from a pile on a chair and wrapping the dead crabs into it. He had his head down trying to keep up with the demand. He didn't even look up when he took Jack's cash, but Jack caught a glimpse of his face. It was at that same stall that Jack saw the ad for the cheap logs at Greenstone Island as there were a pile of leaflets on the stall's table.

In the hospital room Jack realised that the man at the market stall was Ned and another memory was triggered. Jack took out his wallet.

After stories had been told, Jack thanked Ned for saving his life, although Ned insisted it was the red ball that saved his life. A doctor walked in with a clipboard. He greeted the gathered family and then wandered to the side of Ned's bed. "How are we feeling today, Sir... sorry... Mr. Jenkins?" as he checked Ned's pulse against his medical watch.

Ned looked at the reunited family in the room and with his eyes welling up he said, "I'm feeling great. I've never felt better in my life."

Chapter 28

A week later, Ned fully recovered, was emptying a bucket full of crabs onto the beach at Turtle Bay. "There you go my little beauties," as they quickly scurried away across the golden sand. "You did a great job. Hurry along now before your Uncle Ned changes his mind." He then returned to his beach house as he whistled a happy tune.

The beach house had been cleaned up with everything back in its place and a new leather suite. Ned wandered over to the tank. All the aquatic plants have been removed and water drained. At the bottom of the tank was just rocks embedded in sand, except one, the large 'rock' in the middle. Ned pulled the object out. It was very heavy and still concealed in black tarpaulin. Ned placed the object carefully on the kitchen counter. Also on the counter was a jiffy bag and a handwritten note. At the top of the note it said, 'Instructions for Sam'. He folded the note up and put it in the jiffy bag, sealing it.

His mobile phone rang, and Ned quickly picked it up. "Yes, I've got the sample." As he slowly pulled away the black tarpaulin, he revealed a glowing green emerald. "And there's plenty more where this one came from my friend. When's our meeting with the clients? Good, good, yes, I will be there. What's that you say? Three more villas sold. That's super news my friend." Just before Ned put the phone down, he said, "Oh Joey, are we still on for the grande opening next week? Super."

At the end of the call, Ned searched on the kitchen shelf for the card with Maggie's telephone number on it. He made the call as he wandered back to the tank. He observed that some small emeralds had chipped off the large emerald that he had removed from the tank. "Pesky little buggers," he said, describing the crabs just before Maggie answered the phone.

Weeks before, on his way home from San Pengio market, Jack threw the dead crab wrapped in newspaper onto the passenger seat of his truck. As he did so, he noticed three small green stones roll out from the newspaper. He looked at the stones for a while, then put all three in the zipped up part of his wallet.

After Ned's phone call to Maggie, there was another phone call he had to make. It was to the Orphanage in Caracas. He was immediately put through to Sister Margaret, as she was the nun that found the child on the doorstep thirty-four years ago. She remembered it well, it felt like it happened yesterday. She was happy to speak about Maggie as she had treated her as though she was her own. As she described the child, it was as though she was describing the photo that Rosa had shown Ned.

The child in the white blanket, with the green eyes and the small red birthmark on her chin. The birthmark that Ned had seen on the twin with the green eyes when he was sitting in Maggie's kitchen, the birthmark that was still evident on Maggie's chin, as a small mole. After the long phone call, Ned already had a theory about Rosa and the child that got in the way of her future. He vowed he wouldn't tell Maggie, it would be his secret, who would want a mother as evil and cold hearted as Rosa.

Chapter 29

A week after Ned made his phone call to Maggie and the orphanage, a taxi reached the North Coast of Greenstone Island and it drove through row upon row of luxury villas. It had come from the harbour where it had picked the family up from the ferry.

Sam was peering out of a back window. He was so excited as he looked at the swimming pools attached to each villa. "Wow wow wow," is all he could say each time he saw a different villa and another swimming pool.

The taxi eventually pulled up in front of a magnificent white building at least ten storeys high as Sam read the name across the front. 'The Greenstone Grande'. He spotted Mia standing next to L'il Joey at the top of some marble steps.

Joey was dressed in a white suit, as he greeted arriving guests and showed them through the opulent doors. Mia was also dressed in a smart white suit. Sam, Maggie and a clean-shaven Jack exited the taxi. His bandage had been removed, his previous long hair cut. As Jack was retrieving the twins who are strapped in child seats, Mia rushed down the steps to greet them. At the bottom of the steps she extended her hand towards the top of the steps, she had her other hand behind her back. She bowed and said, "Welcome to the Greenstone Grande."

As the family ascended the stairs totally in awe, a

smartly dressed porter collected their luggage from the boot of the taxi. When they reached the top a smiling Joey said, "Welcome my friends." And to Mia, who had followed them back up the steps, "Mia, show our special guests to the presidents suite."

Mia walked to the front of the group, put her hands behind her back and proudly said, "Follow me".

As they were shown through impressive revolving doors, a coach load of holiday makers pulled up. As they descended the coach, the driver changed the destination at the front from Greenstone Island back to Caracus. Amongst the holiday makers were two chattering nuns in their sixties. The same two nuns who were witnesses at Jack and Maggie's wedding, and the same two who were at Jack's memorial. One of them excitedly shook her invitation in the air as she looked at the hotel. "Doesn't it look wonderful, Sister Margaret?" It was their first holiday away from the orphanage in years.

Another distinguished holiday maker descended the coach, a man in his mid-thirties. He was wearing a canary yellow suit with a pink carnation pinned to the lapel. He was with another man in his thirties, a taller man. The taller man pointed to some picturesque mountains in the distance. "Look Felipe," he said, "doesn't it look stunning?"

In the president's suite dressed in a white shirt, tie, black trousers and black jacket, Jack looked out to the panoramic view of the Caribbean Sea. He twisted the pen knife in his hands whilst he spoke on his mobile phone. "Don't forget to tell Mum to set an extra place for thanksgiving this year" "Ok Dad. We will see you all soon. Bye Dad. Love you all too."

Jack put the phone down on a table next to an opened white Ripley's box , the photo of Jack and Ned with the fish, a bunch of keys tagged The Flying Fish, a Greenstone Island leaflet, an opened bottle of Dom Perignon compliments of the management J&N and a handwritten letter.

Jack picked the letter up and read it again. It was from Ned, left in the hotel room on their arrival.

'Dear Jack a.k.a Woody,

It fills me with so much joy to know that you have been reunited with your family. I did enjoy the short time we spent together, especially fishing at the lagoon. I will never forget it; it was the best time of my life. Anyway, I hope you don't mind but I have made you and Maggie the major benefactors in my will (copy enclosed). I'm not getting any younger, and I've got no-one else to leave it to. I can hardly leave it all to a toad, now can I?

Enjoy your stay at the Grande. You are all welcome anytime, and it will always be on the house.

Ned'

Maggie walked into the room. She was wearing a long green silk evening dress that Jack bought for her from JoJo's fashion stores along with some new shoes. Her long auburn hair flowed loosely around her shoulders. She was closely followed by Sam with a twin on either side holding his hands. They were all smartly dressed, Sam was in a black suit and the twins were in pink dresses. In the twin's other hands were the two wooden spoons each with a pink bow attached to it. Jack felt so proud and blessed.

Jack poured two glasses of champagne and

approached Maggie, handing her a glass. He put his hand up and caressed one of Maggie's earrings, an emerald drop earring set in gold. It matched the pendant around her neck. He thought that the jewellers did an exceptionally good job. He looked into her green eyes and said, "Happy belated anniversary to the most beautiful jewel of them all." and kissed her lightly on the lips.

The children giggled. Jack then hugged Maggie close. "Nice watch dad!" shouted Sam. Jack looked at the gold Rolex watch on his wrist.

"Yeh, still can't believe you bought this in Ripley's." Maggie discreetly winked at Sam. "It was a bargain," she said. Sam looked in his own pocket at the cheap Ripley's watch, the watch that Ned instructed him to swap with the Rolex in the jiffy bag.

After their hug, Jack turned to face Sam and the twins. "Who wants to go fishing at the lagoon tomorrow with Ned. I hear the fish are this big?" He demonstrated the size with his hands. The children lifted their arms in a W shape, spoons held high and cheered. "Will we be hooking live maggots, Dad?" asked Sam.

"Probably." "That's awesome."

As they left the hotel room Sam said, "Don't forget your wallet Woody," and laughed. Jack playfully punched him on the cheek.

"I don't need it, son."

Chapter 30

Ned was in a hotel room of the Grande buttoning up a chef's uniform. The mining channel was on TV. He sat on the edge of the bed as he heard a name mentioned, it was Boss. This was one time when Ned didn't want to switch off. There were a couple of mugshots of him, full face, and to the side. Ned listened as the reporter spoke about the collapse of the old mine in Bogotá in which ten miners died because of the lack of health and safety standards, but Ned already knew that. He knew that when Boss confronted him at Turtle Bay that night. He also knew it was the last mine Boss owned, the other ones having dried up over the years. Then suddenly, there was a newsflash as the bulletin went live to a court building in Bogotá.

There were lots of people waving banners outside displaying 'murderer,' 'bring back hanging,' and some banners had photographs of the dead men. There were jeers as a handcuffed Boss was being led from a police van into the court building. A woman was screaming at him from the barrier, as police tried to hold her back. She had three children around her, two boys and a girl aged between eight and twelve. Ned knew that voice and the camera closed in on her. He was horrified when he saw the grotesque face of Rosa. Fifteen years of plastic surgery had taken its toll. Rosa shouted at Boss, "I want half. I will take you to the cleaners!"

Just before Boss was pushed through the court door by an officer, he turned to Rosa and said, "There's nothing left my dear, not a cent." Rosa took off her wedding ring and was about to throw it at him, but decided to keep it at the last minute, as it might be worth something.

Boss then disappeared into the court building. Ned thought he wouldn't be seeing that grinning face for a very long time and he happily turned the TV off. He went to a small fridge and took out a bottle of Greenstone Island mineral water. "Time to turnover a new leaf as they say in good old Blighty," he said, as he opened the bottle and took a swig. He grabbed the chef's hat from the bed, popped it on his head, and did a little jig as he left the room, patting his trouser pocket.

Chapter 31

The hundred seat restaurant was a hive of activity. A calypso band played in one corner of the room and four chefs were cooking on an open grille. Holiday makers and local islanders were sat at tables enjoying their food. A bottle of Pierre Verte wine complimented every table.

Jack and Maggie were looking through the Greenstone Island leaflet and circling villas that they liked. Jack had been commissioned by Ned and Joey to build furniture for the villas. With that, and Mateo taking over management of the shop in San Pengio, the future was looking very bright. A second home at Greenstone Island would be ideal for the family.

"I think I'll give the Flying Fish back to Ned," said Jack. "I'll need a bigger boat if I'm going to be transporting a lot of furniture."

A waiter dressed in a black uniform and a small white apron weaved through the packed tables of holiday makers and islanders. He was carrying five covered plates on a tray. He passed the two nuns. "Sister Margaret, did you remember to bring the travel plug?"

"Oh, stop fussing Sister Mary."

He passed Felipe and the tall man. "Fancy popping some champagne on one of those peaks tomorrow, Felipe?"

"That's an excellent idea." He passed many tables of

the miners, smartly dressed, each spending family time. He passed a table with four young women, the same women who were dancing at Joey's party. One was wearing a diamond heart shaped pendant. She was showing the other women a photo of Flex. He had another tattoo done on his other arm while he had been in prison. It was a pin up of a woman in a red bikini, it was the maid. "He'll be out in 6 months," the maid said excitedly to her friends, "if he doesn't misbehave."

The twins were sitting in their highchairs. They each had a bowed wooden spoon in one hand. Sam perused the busy restaurant. He spotted Mia in one corner of the room who was sitting with five other people. He recognised Joey and her grandmother from the framed photograph on the B&B wall. He looked closer at the three other people. A lady dressed in a vibrant flowing red ball gown, a man sat next to her wore a red bolero jacket, and the other man was in a blue overall. He had a miner's lamp fixed to a band on his head. In disbelief, Sam looked back at Maggie and Jack, who were still looking at the leaflet. Sam took a few deep breaths and looked over again at Mia's table. Now there were just three people- Mia, Joey and her grandmother. Mia looked over at Sam, smiled, opened her hand and lightly blew on it. She released a blue butterfly that flew across the room to Sam. It circled above his head for a short while and then flew out of an open window. "What's the matter Sam?" Maggie asked. "You look like you've seen a ghost."

Sam looked back at Maggie. "No, it was just a butterfly." The waiter arrived at their table with the covered dishes. He gave the twins the smaller dishes, then

Maggie and Jack's, and lastly Sam's. Maggie and Jack took the silver lids off their ordered starter dish to reveal lobster bisque, perfectly seasoned this time. The twins lifted their lids to reveal boneless chicken drumsticks served with mashed potato and peas. Finally, Sam lifted his lid. His dish was wrapped in newspaper. Handwritten on the outside were the words 'I never forget a promise'. Sam looked over to the grille and saw Ned in a chef's hat smiling at him. Sam unravelled the newspaper to reveal a dish of battered fish and chips. He looked closer at the pile of chips; something was glowing underneath them. "What is it son?" asked Jack. The twins started banging their spoons on their silver lids as they watched Sam put in two fingers as though taking out a chip.

"It's a gem of a fish dish," said Sam as he revealed the golf sized green emerald.

Sam held the emerald high in the air and said to Jack "Now Dad, can I have a Gameboy?"

Printed in Great Britain
by Amazon